BLINDED BY
THE LIGHT

BLINDED BY THE LIGHT

R.M. Demeester

Table of Contents

1 6

2 14

3 23

4 32

5 44

6 54

7 66

8 75

9 84

10 94

11 103

12 111

13 124

14 132

15 140

16 149

17 156

18 166

19 175

20 185

21 197

1

After signing my name at the bottom of the medical form, I handed it back to the receptionist. She glanced at it, then looked back at me with a jovial smile. "Da-knee-elle, why don't you take a seat?"

I gritted my teeth to keep from opening my mouth to correct her. A fellow behind me took my spot in line almost impulsively. Gnawing on my lip, I sat down on a hard plastic seat with noticeable signs of wear.

How did I end up with a misspelled name? *Danyelle.* It was an overcomplicated, butchered spelling of an otherwise typical name that my parents had blessed me with.

It was a nuance, I suppose, but my parents' reasoning was that I wouldn't be like everyone else. Then again, I was already different from everybody else. Now I was that particular girl with a weirdly-spelled name. I was also the only one of my siblings whose name wasn't spelled the way it should have been

I reached for a magazine and flipped through it for an article to read, staring blankly at the models in scant clothing on every page. I wouldn't be caught dead in such attire. I closed the magazine and glanced through the other available publications laid out on the table. Why couldn't they stock their minuscule collection with something interesting? A nature or history magazine, perhaps? National Geographic, anyone? Anything to keep my mind off why I was here in the first place. There was a huge chance I was pregnant and the timing couldn't have been worse.

"Danyelle Fitzgerald."

Grateful for a break in celebrity gossip I didn't care about, I tossed the magazine on the table and followed the medical assistant through a lone door. Like the worn chairs in the waiting room, the hallway we ambled down was in dire need of some maintenance. The peeling paint and yellow water stains on the ceiling didn't help my anxiety.

The nurse turned to me, and I couldn't tear my eyes away from her 1980s' perm. "I need you to slip your shoes off so I can take your weight and height." I had to conceal a snicker — she reminded of the photos I'd seen of my mom and aunt in their high school days.

I tucked a strand of my hair behind my ear as I stepped onto the scale. The number wouldn't come as a surprise; I was five foot three and very particular about maintaining a healthy weight so that I wouldn't need to worry about the hassle of losing or gaining weight.

The nurse jotted something down in a folder, which struck me as somewhat odd. With all the technology at our fingertips, why wouldn't she type that information into a computer? It seemed so old-fashioned, so twenty years ago. I enjoyed learning about history but not *living* it.

"Please come this way."

I trudged behind her, down another depressing and drab brown, chipped-paint hallway. When we reached the consultation room, she motioned me to the table. Without another word, she left the room and yanked the door shut behind her. Beads of perspiration dotted my forehead as I tucked my legs underneath me. I glanced around the room at the posters on the bulletin board on the wall across from me. One sign inquired: *Have you had your blood pressure taken lately?* Admittedly, I didn't check my levels as often as I should. My excuse—which wasn't even really an excuse, but more of a way to convince myself that I didn't need to—was my youth. I was twenty-six. I ate well, exercised, and lived an otherwise stress-free life. But there's a history of high blood pressure and heart disease in my family, which should be motivating enough for me to be more conscientious.

I slumped, avoiding eye contact with another poster that made me feel too old. Another reason I never visited the doctor's office was the waiting. But what could I expect? This was a walk-in clinic, after all. And I was here waiting for good news. At least, I hoped it would be. God, if it wasn't good news, what would I do? *I'm too young for this. Please let it be good news!* A lump in my throat grew. I'd been trying to overlook why I'd come here. But the possibility existed—the one thing that would shake up my world. My perfect, undisturbed realm was at risk of blowing up.

I couldn't be pregnant. Yet my period was late, and it was never late.

I rocked back and forth. How could I have been so stupid? I wasn't a heavy drinker. Nonetheless, what was supposed to have been a couple of drinks turned into a huge bender. And I wasn't the impulsive type. Well, I hadn't been, until I'd jeopardized my entire image. Growing up, I had always been the perfect girl. I never got in trouble. I was mature, and I did well in school. As an adult, I paid my taxes on time, saved money, and was responsible. Still, here I was, awaiting my pregnancy results at a walk-in clinic. It had taken me two hours to get here without running into someone who knew me. The perfection everyone expected of me would be shattered if they knew. I'd managed to avoid seeing anyone, but what would happen if the test was positive?

The door opened, and a doctor walked in. He was different from the last one. I preferred consistency. Another doctor who'd never had a conversation with me and could evaluate the results like someone reading mathematical facts off a spread sheet. An intense uneasiness crept up my throat.

"Danyelle?"

I rocked back and forth. "Can you tell me the results? Tell me. I took two tests—one was negative, and the other had a super faint line."

I'd blurted it out in a slightly more callous tone than I'd intended. But I needed to know. I had spent the better part of the last few days studying this on the internet. Those inane stick tests can show false positives. They called them an evaporation line. I just hoped my test was wrong. God, I hoped so.

He glowered at me for a few moments.

"Tell me!" I demanded again, searching his face for an answer.

He puckered his brow. "Miss Fitzgerald, you're not pregnant."

The relief was instant. I felt woozy. "Thank you, thank you. Thank you." I got up to leave, but he coughed coarsely.

"Maybe we could discuss options?"

I stood, dumbstruck. "What options? You said I'm not pregnant."

"There is the possibility of birth control, and of course, there are several options—"

I shook my head, cutting him off. "Thanks, but no thanks," I interrupted as I pushed to leave. Besides, I wasn't that kind of girl.

I came here for one thing. My question was answered, and now I was on my way out. Before I left, I stopped at the counter to pay the consultation fee in cash—I didn't want this showing up on my insurance.

I didn't look around to see if anybody saw me leave the sliding-scale women's clinic. I was ready to put this behind me and pretend the possibility had never even existed. There was a bounce to my step.

Once I made it to my car, I stretched and inhaled the scent of freshly cut grass. It was over, fortunately. I opened the door, sat down, put the key in the ignition, and fastened my seatbelt before pulling away. Halfway down the block, I turned the radio to an oldies country station. I bopped my head to Patsy Cline's "Walkin' After Midnight." Ironically, I embraced today's technology but liked to tune into music of the past as an internal escape. That made me incongruous.

I turned down a random street with no particular destination in mind. My head floundered, lost in its own world. Now that my mind wasn't preoccupied with babies, I was able to think freely about ordinary things. Like what to have for dinner or what museum to visit this weekend. It was one of the perks of being myself.

A white Honda Civic approached the next four-way stop at the same time as I did. The male driver and I made eye contact, and his azure eyes sent a cold shiver down my spine. A car behind me honked, making me jump, and my foot accelerated firmly. So did the other car, and we collided. Another jolt, and my head flung forward and then back.

I swore to myself. The driver who'd honked at me veered around, raising his middle finger at me before speeding out of sight.

At least he could get to where he was going, jerk.

Several feet from me, the man with the annoyed blank stare exited his vehicle. We stood, neither of us saying a word.

He reached into his pocket for his phone, crouched, and snapped a few photos of my front bumper and the surrounding area. The man's eyes were so mesmerizing, I couldn't pay any attention to what was going on. To my dismay, the front headlight was cracked and so was the bumper, but it was still hanging on, if a little crooked. The state of his vehicle was similar: cracked bumper, broken headlight, and the hood was scrunched a bit.

The man frowned. "It's not serious."

"Huh?"

"The damage," he explained, and his eyes softened.

His voice brought me back to reality. "So? Do we call it in?" Not once have I been in an accident, let alone one I caused.

The man shifted his weight from foot to foot thoughtfully. "There's no need to call the police."

I shrugged. "Okay. Why don't we exchange insurance information?"

Again, he shillyshallied. "I don't have the insurance card on me."

I glanced at him. He was avoiding eye contact as precipitation dotted his forehead. Something didn't sit well with me.

"If you don't have insurance information, it might be better for the police to come out and make a report."

"No, no," he stammered. "It's only a fender-bender. No big deal."

Now I was skeptical. "I hit you. Why wouldn't you want my liability coverage to pay for the damage?"

"I just don't want to wait around for the cops, that's all."

I planted my hands on my hips. "This isn't about insurance, is it?" My heart was beating faster. "I don't want to get burned. So, either you have someone bring the insurance info, or I'm calling the authorities." This was my cue to at least jot down his license plate number.

"The truth is . . ." he began, then trailed off.

I ran a hand through my dark brown hair. "I'm listening. We're blocking traffic here, so spit it out."

"I don't have a valid license." He lowered his gaze, and I glared at him. He scraped a hand through his hair, pleading with me without actually begging. And here I was, almost entertaining the idea. My car already needed repairs, and my comprehensive insurance would cover most of it.

"Why are you driving, then?" What I really wanted to ask him was why he was being an idiot, but I'd been the one who'd crashed into him.

He took a deep breath. "Because I'm reckless."

I scoffed.

Without another word, he hurried back toward his car.

Oh, heck no, he wasn't running from this! I followed close behind. "Where are you going?" My hand grasped for my phone, and I quickly took a picture of his license plate. "Do you have any ID on you?"

The man shook his head. "I'll pay for the damage to your car. Just don't call the police."

I opened my mouth to object, but instead asked, "Can I see your ID before entertaining this proposal of yours?"

He retrieved his wallet from his breast pocket, and I grabbed it. He reached to take it back, but I crudely placed my hand on his.

Another car honked as it swerved around us. "I just don't need you pulling a fast one on me, all right?" On the inside, I was screaming at my stupidity. Lately, I had been making foolish decisions. Today was a lucky break, but already, I was once again going against my instincts. Why? Because some guy asked me to?

Searching his wallet, I found a student ID that had expired a few years ago. Ian Fogg. It looked like the same guy, so it wasn't a fake. Before ending the conversation, I glanced at the t-shirt under his coat, emblazoned with the logo of a company. A and D plumbing. That may come in handy if he isn't true to his word.

Ian—the chap now had a name—grabbed a pen and a crumpled receipt from the back pocket of his jeans. He wrote down his name and number and handed it to me. "There, you have my information. Please hold off and let us work out a deal, all right? Look, I have to get to work . . ." he trailed off, giving me puppy eyes.

I took the wrinkled piece of paper, phone in hand, and dialed the number. At this point, I didn't care that we were holding up traffic. He hesitated and opened his mouth to object. "Relax," I said as his phone started to ring. "I just wanted to make sure the number is legit."

He breathed a sigh of relief. "Thank you."

"Just so you know, I still think you are irresponsible."

He bowed his head in shame. "I know."

"I guess that's all. I'll be in touch. We should probably get off the road."

"Yeah. Sorry for the inconvenience." He hurried back to his car.

Before he drove away, I snagged a few photos of the accident scene. I hoped Ian wouldn't compel me to make his life a living hell just for granting him a break.

As I sped away, my mind struggled to convince me I'd made the right decision. He was cooperative, but generally that didn't matter. Often, I was pissed, exasperated, and gave no one a break. Why him? I'd shown unconditional confidence in someone who shouldn't have been driving in the first place. I felt like a substantial fool.

Once again, I'd gone against my instincts. Ian was driving without a license and could have very well just driven away. But he didn't. He was honest. Maybe that was why I'd given him a break? Or maybe because he seemed different, just like me?

2

I left the auto body shop in one of my moods. I was peeved.
How in the world could a cracked bumper and headlight,
even on a brand-new car, cost fifteen hundred dollars? The
collision hadn't been that severe, but then again, I wasn't a
mechanic. A part of me wanted to go to another shop and get
another two or three quotes. But all the reviews online had
raved that this auto shop was the most economical.

After driving a few blocks, I pulled over. Last night after
the crash, Ian and I had exchanged a few messages. I had
mentioned I'd get a quote, and then we could discuss what to
do. I typed in Ian's number. I hadn't added him as a contact,
because we weren't friends. He was just an idiot. Or, we were
both idiots on the road. Either way, I texted him.

Hey. I got a quote for 1500.

Thank God he was cooperating, but the pit in my stomach
didn't agree. My insides were constricting, threatening to
squeeze the life out of me like a python does with its prey.

Ian responded quickly. *Damn, okay . . . I'm off in a few hours,
so I'll call you then.*

I felt the same way he did. If only he had insurance. Sure,
I'd still be out money for my deductible, but I wouldn't have
to part with my money at all if he hadn't been on the damn
road in the first place.

Not bothering to reply to his last text, I drove away. My knuckles were turning white from gripping the steering wheel. Why? What was wrong? Why had I consented to Ian's absurd request? He had no business being on the road, and here I was, stressing.

I tried to wrap my brain around why Ian had distracted me in the first place. It wasn't typical of me to be frazzled, to act so impulsively. I'd crashed into him, which in itself wasn't ordinary. Ian wasn't exceedingly pleasant, but he wasn't discourteous, either. Nothing he said or did should have made me feel sorry for him. It felt supernatural, and that didn't sit well with me — I always had an answer for everything.

My phone rang, snapping me out of my thoughts. My mother's number was displayed on the touch screen.

Mom always called when she was worried or to play twenty questions. My guess was that she'd driven past my house, saw the damage to my car, and was concerned.

Beads of perspiration formed on my temple as I ignored the call.

Soon, my screen indicated a text and asked if I wanted it read to me. Yes.

"Please call me when you get a chance, dear."

How I could explain the accident without lying? Mom had taught me to always tell the truth. If she learned I'd caused an accident, or if she knew that I'd had a pregnancy scare, it'd be the end of the world. Anything that didn't fit into her diminutive box of expectations would change her perspective, and I couldn't have that.

The phone rang again. I let it go to voicemail for the second time, telling myself I'd call her from home. I wasn't looking forward to it. Mom meant well, but these past few days had been difficult, and I didn't want to open that can of worms. I didn't want her to worry.

To distract myself, I turned the radio up. No luck. The DJ, who was usually a favorite, grated on my nerves. My throat felt dry. Insurance and Ian, damn him, were still on my mind.

Reality came crashing back as I pulled up to my two-bedroom, two-bath Victorian house. This was my sanctuary, my pint-sized slice of history. It was one of just a few left on the block. After buying the house last year, my eighty-seven-year-old neighbor told me that some ten years ago, an investor had bought up eight other Victorian houses that had sustained heavy flood damage. He'd bulldozed them and replaced them with the same cookie-cutter dwellings that now littered this long-standing neighborhood. Luckily, my house hadn't sustained much destruction, and the previous owner had been able to restore it.

It was such a shame. These homes held character that these modern houses just didn't possess. How could anything compete with the big, beautiful bay windows and decorative, colored brick work? Why would anyone throw away so much history and replace it with something so dreadful?

Just thinking about it made my skin crawl. I hurried inside and hung my coat on the hook. It had been a long day, and I wanted to lounge and forget it. I felt tired, even though I'd left work ahead of schedule to deal with this insurance fracas and still made it home half an hour earlier.

I sprawled on the couch and turned on the television. A documentary rerun about Cleopatra. Back then, women weren't viewed as powerful, but her intellect had earned her the role of Queen of Egypt. It was certainly fascinating.

My phone rang. Mother, yet again. Not wanting her to think I was intentionally ignoring her, I picked it up.

"Hello?"

"Danyelle! You answered . . ." There was sense of relief in her voice, even as it trailed off. It was coming.

"I was driving." I caught myself. "How are you?" I stood and patrolled the room.

"I just saw your car. Are you all right? What happened? Are you injured?"

I groaned. "Yes, it was a minor fender-bender. Nothing insurance won't cover." Okay, maybe not insurance, but I was leaving out that little tidbit for both our sanities.

It sounded like she was ploughing around, looking for something. "Okay, tell me everything. In case insurance doesn't cover it."

I set the phone down and turned it on speaker. "There is nothing really to tell." My mind raced a million miles an hour. I prodded at my sleeve. "It happened at an intersection. There were no injuries, and insurance will cover it." I just prayed that Ian followed through. Besides, I wanted my car fixed — I still had four more years of loan payments.

"Are you sure?" She was clearly still concerned.

If only I could reach through the phone, hug my mom, and tell her everything was fine.

"You sound a little frazzled, my dear," she added, before giving me a chance to respond.

"I'm fine, Mom, really."

There was some mumbling before she finally said, "All right. But let me know if you start feeling out of sorts."

"You'll be the first call I make, promise."

There was a pause. "Okay. I won't keep you, my darling Danyelle."

"Have a good night."

The moment the call ended felt like bliss. It was easier to maintain this front of the perfect daughter. I lay back on the couch. Ian should be off work by now. I'd done some digging, and the company Ian worked for closed the same time I was usually off each day.

Come summer, work would pick up and become more enjoyable. I could spend fewer hours in the gift shop and more time as a tour guide. I knew the museum like the back of my hand. Pioneer life was intriguing, and I looked forward to sharing my knowledge.

Which reminded me of the few orders I needed to finish up. While I loved working at the museum, it didn't pay well. It was a shame more value wasn't put on olden times. But there was still a niche market, as I saw a steady stream of people searching for costumes from different eras. Even when business was slow, I kept busy creating other customary apparel.

A client came every few months wanting a variation of garb from the Wild West period. The "Old West," as they called it, was one of my favorite eras.

I climbed the stairs to the second story. To the left was my master bedroom with a built-in desk and shelving area. It was rustic and I loved it. To my right was the guest/sewing room. Eventually, it might become a large walk-in closet, but that would mean losing a bedroom. Two-bedroom houses sold for more money than homes with just one bedroom. If I turned this into a one-bedroom, it would be strictly for me. But would I stay here for the long term?

I had to stop letting my mind wander. I retrieved the red gingham dress from its hanger. The garment was nearly finished.

Just as I began sewing, my phone vibrated. I set the costume on the table and reached for the phone.

I just got home. Is that the only quote you got?!?

I clenched my jaw. *Yeah, from Star and Moon's Autobody.*

If he could find a cheaper place with great reviews, then cheers to him.

Shit!!!!! Okay. He replied quickly with a second text. *Do you mind if I have someone look at it? I didn't think it'd cost that much.*

My heart sped up. It *was* a lot of money, which is why we have insurance — or at least, most of us did.

Sure, as long as they are qualified.

I didn't want anyone other than a trained auto body mechanic to look at it. But he should have a chance; I wanted to resolve this problem amicably.

He's legit.

I wanted to tell him that I'd rather just pay my deductible and he could worry about his own damn car, but I didn't want to be that person.

How soon? Once again, going against my instincts. It was so not me.

Where do you live? He can come over right now.

Goosebumps speckled my arms. I didn't want him or his friend at my place. *How about I come to you?* That way, I could turn on the location finder, in case something happened. I was a pessimist. Or maybe overly cautious. Or both.

Okay, 266 Wright Street.

Great, I'll leave right away. Be there in ten minutes.

It was only a few blocks away. Was it just a coincidence he lived in the same area? Maybe it wasn't his house — maybe he was renting? Maybe there was more to him then met the eye?

I knew the house. It wasn't quite as old as mine and still had its original brick. I had an eye for that kind of detail.

Before leaving my house, I sat in the car for a few minutes. If I showed up too quickly, he'd wonder if I lived nearby. I couldn't have him speculating.

But when I finally pulled up to the residence, I was disenchanted. The brick had been painted white. Why would someone do that? It wasn't my house, but it was disheartening that someone would destroy a piece of the town's antiquity.

Ian sauntered down the driveway before I had a chance to get out of my car. He wore a plain, form-fitting white t-shirt and knee-length jean shorts. Under his t-shirt, I could tell his abs and biceps were well defined. At least he was a fit, fine-looking guy, which helped make up for his irresponsible behavior. It sounded awful, but it was true.

"Hey," he said.

"Hi," I replied. "Is this your place?"

He shrugged. "I rent a room downstairs."

I nodded. "It's a nice residence."

"Sure," he agreed, glancing back at the building. "Nice, I guess."

I stood there for an awkward moment. I wasn't good at small talk, and it showed.

"So, where is your friend?" I honestly needed to figure out how my car would be fixed, not get myself smitten with a guy who is clearly more trouble than he is worth.

"He's grabbing a coffee around the corner. I should have asked him to get you one."

I shrugged.

"Sorry again," he said, out of nowhere.

"It was an unfortunate misadventure," I said dismissively, "and not what either of us needed."

His laugh was halfhearted. "Tell me about it." Then he lowered his voice to a whisper. "Just one more thing in my shitty life."

So, was he down on his luck, or was he making shitty choices? Either way, it sucked. It wasn't my problem, but a twinge of sympathy developed for him. Why?

"I get it," I told him, even though I really didn't. "Everybody has downs."

He looked at me, then at my car, and back at me. "Other than this mishap, I'd assume you are currently not having a down."

"For right now, yeah. But things can change. Unexpected things transpire all the time."

Ian shifted from one foot to the other, checking his watch and clearly wondering where the hell his friend was when he stopped and looked at me. "Maybe you could tell me why the garage quoted so high?"

I turned to head back to my car. "I'll grab the estimate."

"Seven hundred for a bumper, two hundred for headlight replacement." He read out loud. "This shouldn't be more than a couple hundred dollars in parts." Then he mumbled something about a fender. It was excessive? He handed the form back to me. "Where did they come up with those numbers? I shouldn't be complaining, but damn."

I had no idea what to say. Just let him rant, if it made him feel better.

"Okay, he's here."

I turned to see an older gentleman exiting his vehicle. He stopped short of my car.

"Is this the car?" he shouted.

Ian walked past me to stand with the other man by my vehicle. "Yeah. The shop is saying it'll cost fifteen hundred to fix it."

He looked the car over carefully. "Bumper, fender, and light is about three to four hundred in parts. One to two hundred in labor. I could fix this for six hundred, easily."

"Are you a mechanic?" I asked.

The man lifted his glasses and stared, almost like he was studying me. "Yes, ma'am, I am. Been one for twenty-five years next Monday." He patted Ian's shoulder. "I've known this *kid* for nearly as long."

He handed Ian a coffee and me a business card. "I gotta go. If you need those repairs, give me a shout. Ian is good on his word."

"Thanks," I replied, tucking the card in my pocket as the guy drove away.

Ian took a sip of his beverage. "Do you want anything to drink?" he asked. "I hate to sit here and drink alone."

I ignored him. "Where does your friend work?" He'd been in and out so quickly, I hadn't even gotten his name.

"Waylon has his own shop."

I grimaced. "Why didn't you take my car there?"

Ian inhaled and exhaled heavily. "It's on the other side of the river. I just assumed you wouldn't, well, you . . ." He looked like he couldn't find the right words.

I blinked at him. *Over the river, huh? In the ghetto? Is that what he meant?* I almost laughed. "You assumed I was too good for the ghetto?"

He blushed. "Sorta, yeah. You're driving a new car."

"Well, you assumed wrong." I smiled. "I could assume you are a careless jerk or many other things, but I won't. "

He swallowed.

"I'm curious, though," I continued. "Why were you driving without a valid license?"

"Unpaid tickets," he admitted, looking sufficiently embarrassed. "I lost my job and couldn't pay them. Now I got this new job, and I've been slowly paying them off to get my license back. But the problem is, I can't work without driving."

"I see. Well, I should go," I said.

"So, will you use Waylon?"

"Fine. As long as my car gets fixed."

"Thanks." He stopped, blushing again. "I never got your name."

"Danyelle."

"Okay, thanks, Danyelle. Give me some time to come up with the funds. It's just been tough."

I sighed. "All right, but I should go now. Take care, okay?"

He walked me to my car, then nodded toward the driver's side window. "You stopped at the coffee shop around the corner? "

I looked into my vehicle to see the distinctive cup sitting in my console. Damn. "No, that was earlier."

"Do you work around here?"

"No, why?"

He laughed. "I just frequent Hank's Café every so often and have never seen you."

"I go there once in a while if I'm in the area." I couldn't tell him I lived here.

"Anyway," he said, backing away from the vehicle. "I won't keep you. Have a good night."

"You too. Bye." I turned and got into my car. I felt better than I had before I'd come. Ian seemed like a nice guy. A little rough around the edges, sure, but decent.

3

Over the past few days, I had been stopping at Hank's Café more than usual. I stood in line, my feet aching after another busy day. It had been unusually hectic at the gift shop. They'd offered a "buy one, get one free" admission special, not to mention it was spring break and all the students were out of school. The youngsters came in crowds, making noise. I had to juggle keeping an eye out for shoplifting and ringing in orders. It was days like today when I wanted to ask for a raise.

Much to my dismay, the line leading up to the counter moved at a snail's pace. At work, I often had speed tests. My manager expected quick, efficient service — he didn't like people who dilly-dallied when there were things to do, and even worse, those who complained about being tired. I wondered how many people here passed their speed check, though I would guess not many, the way they were going. I checked my watch before turning back to the till. All I wanted was a tea, but maybe the long, drawn-out line was a sign? My mind was starting to wander, which wasn't like me.

A metallic taste filled my mouth. I couldn't deny it — I was thinking of Ian. His rough-around-the-edges persona was intriguing. I could have stayed longer and kept talking to him, but I'd gotten nervous. He wasn't afraid of my questions. He was open, although maybe reluctantly, and he didn't beat around the bush. Unpaid parking tickets could happen to anyone—just like my becoming distracted and crashing into him could have happened to anyone. It wasn't like me and probably wouldn't happen again.

Finally, I reached the till.

"What can I get for you?"

A lump formed in my throat. For a moment, I was at a loss for words. "Um, a tea."

"What kind?" She pointed to the list on the board behind her. My face was getting hot. I've frequented Hank's enough to memorize their menu.

"Green tea with a hint of cream. And can I have a cup with a lid? I don't want to burn myself like I did a few months ago. Thanks."

I handed her a bill before moving to the right while she took the next order. A minute or so later, another employee handed me a steaming cup. I beamed. The aroma was so satiating.

I settled at a table by the window, where I could observe the cars zooming by. It was a beautiful day. The sky was clear and blue. The branches on the trees barely moved. There was no wind—everything was at a standstill.

After finishing my drink, I left the cafe. Upon reaching my car, an all-too-familiar Honda drove up and parked one row up and three stalls over.

My body froze. One hand gripped the car handle, but my gaze was fixated on the Honda. The door popped open and Ian exited. My legs trembled. I had just been thinking about him! Actually, I'd probably come here because, on some level, I wanted to see more of him.

He walked away without making eye contact and headed for the door. I debated going back inside, but I didn't have a convenient excuse. Darn.

Maybe I should just go home. Here I was stalking him. Not to mention I didn't know if he even liked me, or just saw me as the idiot who crashed into him. I didn't know what was wrong with me. This budding curiosity was going to make me go mad.

Before I could make a decision on what the hell to do, Ian came back out the door almost immediately, walking briskly toward his Honda. I forced myself to get in my own car.

Too late—he spotted me.

"Hey, Danyelle!" he shouted.

I stood back up, glancing over at him. "Oh, hey Ian. I didn't see you…"

He sported a crooked smile. "Fancy meeting you here. I saw your car in the parking lot yesterday, as well. This must be a favorite place, right?"

My face grew hot. "I could say the same about you." No need to tell him I'd started coming here in hopes of running into him.

He bounced from foot to foot. "I forgot my wallet."

I took note of his jumpiness. "Oh?"

"Yeah." He looked away awkwardly, then started heading back toward his car.

"I was about to get myself a tea. Would you like to join me?"

I nearly gasped at my outburst. I found my confidence! From where?

Ian turned and walked back over, unbuttoning the top of his shirt. "Sure."

I held back a chuckle as I smiled at him. He acted so cute, almost innocent. It reminded me of the boys in junior high, way back when. Taylor, my first "boyfriend," if you could even call him that, had often written sappy notes to me, and blushed every time I passed him in the halls. He never worked up the courage to ask me to a dance.

"Weren't you getting your wallet?" I asked.

"Oh, yeah." His face turned a deep red. "Preoccupied, you know?"

His car had been fixed, but it looked incredibly messy. Even from a distance, I could tell the interior he was rummaging through was full of junk, food wrappers, and other miscellaneous things I couldn't identify. I held back a groan. How did someone deal with that without going crazy? He closed the door, wallet in hand, and noticed me staring.

"You got your car fixed."

He nodded. "Sort of." He gulped, looking chagrined.

"Sorta?" I asked. "Unless I need to get my eyes checked, it looks pretty fixed."

"I got a bumper from the junkyard and attempted to fix it myself."

I raised an eyebrow. Why hadn't he asked Waylon? They were friends, weren't they? The bumper appeared to be on properly. The hood and light were fixed, as well. Yet he hadn't mentioned that. He was likely too embarrassed. Or maybe Waylon had fixed it, but he wouldn't tell me because he didn't have insurance?

"Ready?" Ian asked.

I nodded, and we approached the entrance together. I tucked my hair behind my ears. Hopefully, the staff wouldn't say anything about my earlier visit. That awkwardness would surely cause some unneeded discomfort.

Several feet away from me, Ian stared down at his feet as he walked. He seemed rather engrossed. There was something about him . . . I couldn't put my finger on it. The way he watched, moved, communicated—I couldn't relate. Ian Fogg was a big question mark to me, and I wanted to figure out what about him had me so intrigued.

He ordered a coffee, then looked over at me, his hand trembling. "What do you want?"

"I'll get my own."

He gritted his teeth, turned, and told the lady behind the counter that was all. After he paid, he stood to the side as I made my order. I didn't want his money. I really just wanted him to fix my car.

And I wanted a convenient excuse to get to know him better. I hoped I wasn't sending mixed signals.

After I received my second mug of tea, we took a seat by the window. The chairs were rigid and uncomfortable. The décor in general was mismatched, odd, and very quaint.

"I would have gotten it," Ian whispered.

"I know." Now I felt guilty. "I'm not used to nice gestures."

"That's a shame." Ian's voice trailed off, and his face contorted in a grimace.

"I appreciate the offer, though." I stared at his hand, wanting to reach over and caress it. I stopped myself, not wanting to give him the wrong idea. He still needed to pay to fix my car. But even that seemed wrong, because I'd smashed into him.

My resolve was slipping. I was thinking irrationally. He wasn't even supposed to be on the road, because he didn't have insurance. I had to keep reminding myself of that. Yet I wanted to give him a break, even if it was at my own expense. Nonetheless, six hundred dollars was around the price of my deductible. If he had insurance, I would have had to cover it myself. I groaned. No wonder I felt so conflicted. My mind had to shut up before I made another outlandish comment.

"Are you okay?" Ian stared at me with jaded eyes. His lip curled and it seemed like he was struggling to calm his jaw.

I smiled. "I'm fine."

He reached into his pocket for his cell phone. After a bit of scrolling, his gaze met mine. "So it looks like Waylon has some time to fix your car in the next hour. I'd like to get that out of the way, if you don't mind."

"Right now?"

"Yeah. Or should I tell him another time?"

"No, tonight is fine." I didn't have the heart to tell him about my long day and my plan to go home and crawl under the covers.

"Okay, great." He smiled, his posture relaxed. He seemed more serene. Maybe he was like me in the sense that he didn't like to keep things unresolved. My car remaining unfixed stressed me out.

We hurried to finish our beverages before leaving.

"You can follow me," he said, as we headed out of the café.

"All right."

I trailed him out of the parking lot, expecting him to drive to the other end of the city, but he took the exit onto the freeway. I kept a fair distance behind. I'd already checked on the GPS how to get to Waylon's shop.

Even with the speed limit, going through downtown was quicker. Maybe he was worried about his gas mileage? All the idling at traffic lights burned fuel faster than highway driving. While I was frugal, I also liked to get where I needed to as quickly as possible.

The exit he took seemed wrong, too. Was he new to the city? Or was he taking me on a detour for the heck of it? Maybe I had just not considered the many routes to that part of the city. There I was, trying to alter my judgements again. There were many ways, I was sure, but only one made sense to me.

Soon, we pulled up to the auto shop. It was a little run-down. The sign on the façade was faded, and the landscaping left much to be desired — dead flowers hung loosely over the rotting wood pots, and grass was overgrown in some areas and had dried patches in others. I kept my mouth shut as I got out of my car and walked over to Ian.

"Here we are," he announced.

I gnawed at my lip.

"We're here," Ian repeated.

"I know." My response came out a little more curtly than I'd expected.

Ian puckered his brow but didn't reply. Instead, he walked up to the front door and knocked on it. Moments later, Waylon came out in a plain white tee and ripped jeans. He and Ian exchanged a few words before he turned toward me.

"Hello!" Waylon called.

"Hi!"

Ian shadowed him. "How long will this take? I really want to get this over with."

Waylon shrugged. "By tomorrow morning."

I rubbed the back of my neck, biting down on my upper lip. I was having serious second thoughts. Maybe I should have gone through my insurance and just paid the deductible. The run-down shop, the nonchalant owner, and this entire arrangement felt sketchy. However, it was a legit shop—I'd looked it up.

"Can I give you a ride home?" Ian asked.

I stared at him like he was speaking a foreign language. "Huh?"

"While your car is getting fixed. Unless you have another way home?"

I swallowed hard, debating if it was a good idea to get into the car with him—practically a stranger. A stranger who didn't even have a driver's license. I could call for a taxi, but I knew it would cost an arm and a leg to get all the way across the city, and I didn't want to hang out in this area any longer than I had to.

"Is that okay?"

"Sure," I conceded.

As soon as I got into his car, my stomach twisted.

"So what's your address?" He paused, holding up his phone. "Or do you want to just put it in my GPS?"

I instantly swore to myself. I couldn't tell him where I lived! I'd already told him I wasn't from the area.

"The café is fine."

He gawked at me. "Why?"

I looked away.

"Okay, if you don't want me to have your address, that's totally fine. But are you sure?"

"I don't live far from you. I only said I didn't because I was nervous," I replied, too anxious to look at him.

My body began to tremble. My heart raced so quickly, a pain formed in my chest. Where did that come from? It felt like something was weighing me down.

"Danyelle?" Ian shook my shoulder. "Are you okay?"

I've got to go. I told myself, but I was too shaky to move. I began to count. "One. Two. Three. Four." I took a deep breath in and out every count of four and felt my nerves begin to settle.

The last time I'd trembled like that was the morning after the New Year's Party. I'd had a lot to drink, that's all. This time was different. Maybe it was just the load of stress—with work, the car, the pregnancy scare? I needed to take it easy. That was it.

"Are you okay?" Ian probed again.

I glanced into his flustered eyes. "I'm fine. Sorry." I gave him my address and leaned back in my seat, still focused on my breathing.

He drove relatively slowly, and I risked a glance over at him. His face had softened a bit. The beginning of crow's feet marked their place at the corners of his eyes and temple. He appeared older—maybe early thirties? Yet he wasn't greying. Nevertheless, he was an attractive man.

"Sorry again," I finally said, to break the silence.

He glanced over at me and a slight smile crossed his face. "As long as you're okay. I was worried I did something to offend you."

I shook my head. "No. It's nothing." I looked away.

He chuckled. "I was thinking you might have second thoughts about leaving your car with Waylon." He paused. "The structure is somewhat tattered, but I promise he does a great job."

I nodded. Hearing him acknowledge my inner fears without my actually having to tell him what they were made me feel a bit better.

"How did you and Waylon meet, anyway?" I'd been accused of not minding my own business before—it was a trait I'd inherited from my mother. But how else would I know, if I didn't just ask him?

Ian's body stiffened briefly. "Waylon took me under his wing when I got here. He gave me a job and a place to live." Waylon said he knew Ian for a long time. So how long is a long time and how old was Ian.

"So he's a nice guy. But why didn't you get him to fix your car?"

"Because." He paused. "Have you ever changed a tire?" he asked abruptly.

"No. Why?"

"You should learn."

I bit my lip, feeling slightly offended. "I don't need to learn when I can have someone do it for me."

Ian frowned. "Sorry." He clenched the steering wheel.

"What does that have to do with him not fixing your car?" He was avoiding my question, and it pissed me off.

"I just don't like relying on people. I didn't mean to offend you. I only asked because I wanted to know what you'd do if you had a flat."

"I guess." But why didn't he just ask me that question without beating around the bush, making me drag the answer out of him?

"Forget I said anything." Ian looked away. "We're coming up to your block."

I felt like a fool as Ian pulled up to my house. "Here we are."

"Thanks, Ian."

"Have a good night."

He drove off as soon as I got out of his car. I went inside, lounged on my couch, and turned the television to the History Channel. I kept thinking about Ian. I decided to text him to thank him for the ride. We had kind of ended things on a bittersweet note.

4

When I drove to Waylon's shop, my car came back fixed, just as Ian had promised. It seemed looks could be deceiving — the entire night my car was in Waylon's hands, I felt anxious. I swore I had lucid dreams of driving around town with my supposedly new bumper dragging on the concrete. I had texted Ian a few times the past couple days, and his responses were short. I guessed that meant the end of our contact.

I moped around my house, trying to keep my mind on something else, until thankfully, my friend Kiera texted me. We'd been friends since high school but hadn't hung out recently. The last time I talked to her, she had a boyfriend who was isolating her from all her friends. She wasn't even there for me when I needed her. Now she was letting me know that she'd left him.

I was elated to hear that bit of good news, especially after the week I'd had. Kiera was the person I always used to go to when I needed a listening ear. She also told really good stories. She was a bartender and always had lots to say about crazy drunks at her work. She was also great to talk to about fashion. I often used her as my muse for my outfits.

What are you doing? she texted.

I gnawed on my fingernail. I hadn't told her about my little fender bender and certainly nothing about Ian, or not going through insurance, or any of the crazy thoughts I'd had.

Lying around, might watch a documentary. I'm not sure yet.

I hadn't watched much television the past week or so. On a scale from one to ten, with ten being the highest, my stress level was easily a nine. My life could have been so much worse, but I wasn't used to things being out of my control.

Want company? Kiera texted back.

Part of me wanted to say no and just continue moping, but the other part of me, the rational part of me, screamed yes. Kiera would be just the person, if she wasn't still hung up over her break up, to listen to my boy drama. I half-heartedly laughed at how petty that sounded. I was acting like a teenage girl. But in reality, I hadn't seen her in forever, and I was just in the mood to dish. I needed someone to hear me.

Sure. The front door will be open.

Care if I bring some wine? Kiera asked.

The pit in my gut screamed like it was in pain. I hadn't had a drop since the pregnancy scare. The more that I tried to replay the night over, I still couldn't piece together what all I'd done in those six or seven hours. I had been at one friend's house and somehow ended up at another friend's house for a party. I'd been so out of it, I couldn't even be sure it wasn't longer.

Well, is that a yes? I have a bottle of cabernet with our names on it! Kiera texted again.

I couldn't tell her no — she would ask me why, and I didn't want to explain about the New Year's party and all the alcohol and the pregnancy scare. I was still bitter about her not being there for me when I'd called the next morning.

Sure. I would just have to ration myself or not drink at all. Not that I would find myself in that position again; I just didn't want to risk it.

Okay, girl. I'll be there soon.

What I really wanted was not to think about wine or parties or any of that stuff. But Kiera would have other plans.

She wasn't necessarily a partier, but she liked to spend a night in, like me, drinking a couple of glasses of wine and hanging out. She and I were in a few university classes together, so we did share similar interests, but lately her focus had changed. *She* had changed. She dropped out during the last year of her master's when she met her now ex. But I hoped today I'd see a glimpse of the Kiera I knew and loved.

I put the phone down and unlocked the front door. I had security alarm systems hooked up in case someone unsavory came around. I tidied the living room and fluffed up my pillows. My life might have been chaotic these past few weeks, but I had an image to live up to: the put-together friend. At times, it was a chore, and I almost said screw it.

Soon after, from my bay view window, I saw Kiera's flashy red Mustang pull up. She opened the door and leaned over toward the passenger seat. Her high-heeled shoe peeked out of the driver-side door.

She retrieved the promised bottle of wine and ambled up the walkway to my front door. Her tight red strapless silk dress ended a few inches above her knees. I hoped she wasn't planning to go out clubbing, because I had no intention of changing out of my loose attire.

She opened the door. "Hey, Dany."

I stepped toward her and pulled her into a hug. "You're looking good, Kiera."

"You look like you just crawled out of bed."

"Nah, I just changed when I got home from picking up my car."

Kiera raised an eyebrow. "Your car? What happened to your car?"

My face grew hot. "Uh . . . fender bender."

Her grin spread from cheek to cheek. "Did you hit somebody?"

I looked away, and my cheeks burned so intensely, it almost felt like my face was melting. "Kind of."

She shrieked into laughter. "You did not! Was he hot?"

She had me trapped. "Um . . . he was pretty attractive, I guess. But that wasn't why I crashed into him. I just had a bad day and wasn't paying attention. And . . ." I stopped myself. Did I really want to tell her the story about what followed? I did want her advice on where my relationship with Ian might go from here.

"And?" Kiera said, then quickly stood. "What we need is a glass of wine, because this is a story I gotta hear."

I opened my mouth to object but decided on one glass. I had no way out. Kiera wouldn't just drop this. She would want all the details.

She returned with a set of glasses and passed one to me. "Here. Now, details."

I didn't want to tell her about the pregnancy scare yet, so I skipped that part and lied. "I was leaving work after a shitty day, and we both entered the intersection. Neither of us was going, but he started moving first, and I wasn't paying attention and crashed into him."

There was an awkward pause before Kiera spoke up. "And?"

"We were blocking traffic, and he didn't have insurance, and —"

"Wait, hold up. He didn't have insurance? What did the police say?"

I pulled uncomfortably at the collar of my shirt. "I didn't call the police." My throat felt dry.

Kiera's mouth opened wide. "What?"

"I can explain." I really couldn't, but I had to say something. "I felt bad, because I shouldn't have been driving."

She waved her arm. "Hold on, Danyelle. Hold on one second. You give nobody breaks if they are in the wrong. It's illegal to drive without insurance, and you know it."

"It worked out. He paid for my car to get fixed." I blurted.

She rolled her eyes. "Do you know how easily he could have given you a fake number, or he could have denied the whole thing even happened? You're just lucky he was honest."

"I did ask for ID, and I got his license plate number and pictures of the scene." I paused. "But you're right. It was a lapse in judgement."

Kiera polished off her glass of wine and retrieved the opened bottle from the kitchen. I hadn't even touched mine. "Now, what possessed you to *trust* this guy?" she called from the kitchen.

I cleared my throat. "I don't know. There was something about him. There's *still* something about him I can't get out of my mind."

She returned from the kitchen and plopped back down beside me. "You like him? Like, *like* him?"

"Yeah, I think I do." I admitted it aloud for the first time. I did like him. Even if I didn't know him that well. But I'd gotten into a car with him — a complete stranger — and he knew where I lived. He was mysterious yet an honest man, because he kept his word. So maybe that is why I was interested.

She took a swig of her newly poured drink. "Well, tell me about him. There has to be something spectacular about him for you to be attracted to him. We all know you don't go for someone based on looks, and him having no insurance wouldn't have made a good impression."

I laughed. "His name is Ian. And I wasn't impressed, you got that right. Well, not at first." I picked up the glass and took a small sip. "Once my car was fixed, I'd intended for us to go our separate ways. And now that I have my car back, it might just be that way." I realized there was dismay to my voice. "Only, I don't know if I want that."

Kiera polished off her second glass of wine and smiled devilishly. "Then invite him over?"

"Huh?" Then, the panic set in. "No, no. I can't do that!"

She frowned, clearly disappointed. "Fine." She stood and pulled me up next to her. "Why don't you go get changed and we'll go out. We should have a little fun, because you look like you need a break. Maybe meet a hot guy like this dude you hit?"

"Fine," Only I didn't want to go to a bar or night club. I wanted to play catch up after so long. "How about a nice restaurant? I'm in the mood for something exotic."

"Yeah, sure, fine." The grin on her face suggested she probably had somewhere else in mind.

I wouldn't finish my wine if I was going to be driving, so I put it aside and excused myself to my bedroom. I hadn't planned on going out tonight, but I missed her, and I missed spending time with her.

I changed into a short-sleeved, low-cut dress. It wasn't as revealing as Kiera's, but I didn't want to be that undressed while out with someone with almost zero filters. I sat at my vanity and quickly put a layer of cerise on my lips and a bit of mascara on my lashes and ran a brush through my hair. A little went a long way.

When I returned to the living room, Kiera had a huge smile on her face. "What's up?" I asked, apprehensive.

She kept smiling, refusing to say anything. Then I saw my phone in her hand.

"Kiera, what did you do?"

Kiera grinned and sat my phone face down on the coffee table. "I've got to go." She replied, grabbing the bottle. "My ride will be here soon. I'll pick up my car tomorrow."

"What did you do? Kiera?"

She passed me on her way to the door and shot me a wink. "Have fun with Ian."

"Kiera!"

But she was already headed down the front walk. I sat down and reached for my phone. There had apparently been several back-and-forth exchanges in the ten minutes I was upstairs.

Hey, what's up? Kiera had typed to Ian.

A few minutes later he had responded, *I just got home from work and was going to grill up some eggplant and steak.* So he liked eggplant. I did as well, but had never had it with steak. I'd have to try it sometime.

How about you come over and hang out?

Oh God. Why? Kiera, why? I wanted so badly to text him back and tell him it wasn't me, but reading over the next string of messages, it was clearly too late.

Okay. There was another message from him shortly after. *I thought after you got your car, there would be no more contact.*

I'm bored.

God damn it, Kiera.

I didn't expect you to want to hang out, but sure.

She had sent a smile emoticon.

Alright, I'll be there soon.

That message had been sent five minutes ago. I stirred restlessly on the couch. I should have known Kiera would have pulled something like this. She always told me I needed to get out and have fun. I haven't dated much, and she'd tried many times to hook me up, but to set up a date — or whatever this was going to be — was too much. What was I going to say when he got here? "Hey, I also like eggplant?" God, no. Stupid, stupid. I wasn't prepared for this. Was I going to make a fool of myself?

A knock at the front door startled me, but then I realized it had to be Ian. I inhaled and exhaled a few times and headed for the door. My hand shook on the doorknob.

Here goes nothing.

Ian stood on the front porch in a plain t-shirt and a pair of jeans. I realized what I was wearing and what kind of message I was giving, and I made a mental note to get back at Kiera for this little set-up.

"Hey," Ian said awkwardly.

"Come in," I offered, stepping aside.

He nodded out toward the street. "Whose car?"

I sighed. "My friend Kiera's. She was too drunk to drive home, so she got a ride."

He stepped in and looked around. "Nice place."

Just the other day, I'd been too afraid to give him my address. Now here I was inviting him — not by my choice — into my house. "Thanks. Would you like anything to drink? Eat?"

Ian replied with a quiet, "No." He took off his shoes and followed me awkwardly into the living room. I motioned for him to sit down, which he did.

We sat in silence for a few moments. "So, how have you been?" I finally asked.

"I've been good. Just tired after a long day at work."

"What do you do at work?" I asked. It seemed like a safe topic to discuss, since I didn't know what else to ask.

"I'm a plumber. I install sinks and toilets mostly."

"So, I take it you went to school for that." I remembered the student ID he had in his wallet.

"Yeah, I worked two years as a cook to save for tuition."

"No student loans?" I inquired.

Ian leaned forward, planting his elbows on his knees. "No. I was always taught to only pay for things with cash. Debt can cripple you faster than anything. It's bad enough that I have tickets to pay off."

"I understand." I then quickly changed the subject. "Waylon did a good job on my car." I felt anxious, unsure of how to communicate with Ian. It was easy through text, but in person, things were so different.

"I told you he did a good job." Ian smiled. He must think highly of Waylon, because whenever his name was mentioned, it seemed to loosen him up.

"That you did."

He shuffled in his seat, his ears turning a deep red. "I'm sorry about the other day."

"What?" I looked at him as if he had grown a second head. "About what?"

"The disagreement in the car. About insulting you for not knowing how to change a tire."

I lifted an eyebrow. I had forgotten all about that petty debate. "It's nothing to be sorry about. It would do me good to learn how to change a tire, honestly. Maybe you can show me sometime."

Ian's face softened and he let out a small smile. "For sure."

I stood. "Are you sure you don't want anything to eat? I did catch you when you were about to make dinner."

Ian shook his head.

My hands were planted firmly on my hips. "Now, don't be shy."

Ian glanced at me and opened his mouth to speak but didn't.

"I have a few steaks in the fridge," I suggested, "or maybe we can have a campfire in the backyard and roast hot dogs or something."

"A campfire sounds nice." He paused, then added in a whisper, "I didn't have those back home with all the snow."

"Back home?"

He jumped, like he hadn't meant to speak out loud. "Alaska. But it's been years. Not since my parents died."

"I'm sorry."

Ian stood straight up. "It's fine. So, how about that campfire? Good idea."

I forced a smile, leading the way out back. He was from Alaska — quite different from here. I don't even recall the last time we had snow. Winter here was cool, at best. But how easily he'd changed the subject was a little jarring. Did he have a poor relationship with his parents before they died?

As we passed through the kitchen, I grabbed some matches and we headed into the back yard. I had a pretty large lot, considering how congested the rest of the city was.

"Would you grab some logs from over there?" I pointed to the stack in the corner of my yard.

"Okay," he said, and returned a few minutes later with a huge armful of wood. "Where do I put it?"

"In the fire pit." I pointed to that as well.

After he set the logs in the pit, I rearranged them around some carefully placed pieces of scrunched-up newspaper. With my strategic pile in place, I took out a match and lit it. Ian flinched as he took a step back. Soon, the campfire was ablaze.

"I'll grab some lawn chairs," I said, walking to the side of the house to retrieve them.

When we were both seated, I noticed Ian staring off into the distance. "What's on your mind?"

Ian startled. "I was just thinking, that's all."

A slight chill shot up my back as my curiosity crept up. "So, how was Alaska?"

"Cold," he replied, his tone just as frigid. "I'm glad to be somewhere warm."

"Me, too," I agreed, trying to lighten the mood.

"How long have you lived here?" Ian asked.

"All my life." I went on to explain that I'd never really gotten around, rarely traveled outside the city, and named the school I'd gone to. He sat there nodding, apparently engaged, and rubbing his hands together over the quickly rising flames.

"That's good," came his simple response. He didn't talk much, I noticed. Maybe he was just a man of few words. I could work with that, I thought.

"You didn't send those texts for me to come over, did you?" Ian asked out of the blue. He didn't look at me, but just stared into the fire.

For the life of me, I couldn't muster a response. How would he know that?

"I'll take your silence as a yes. The texts were blunt, and from hanging out with you, your actions don't match." Before I could object, he held up his hand. "No, it's alright. It's not a bad thing," he explained. "It was just an observation." He yanked his pants at the knee and leaned back, his arms crossed.

I lowered my gaze. "Yeah, I was talking with a friend and you kind of came up. She thought I needed to get out, so she took it upon herself to set this up."

"I'm sorry I said I'd come over."

"No, no," I added frantically. "I'm glad you came over. I'm having a good time. Aren't you?"

Ian nodded. "Yeah, it's nice."

"You don't say much, do you?"

He ran his hand through his hair. "I usually do a lot of listening."

He wasn't lying there. Tonight, I had done easily eighty percent of the talking. I had openly shared more with him than he had with me. If anything, he'd avoided a lot of topics. It made me wonder what he didn't want to share. What about Alaska, beside it being cold, did he resent? Maybe he didn't grieve his dead parents, or maybe he'd had a bad childhood. Whatever it was, he'd shut me down. It wasn't like he owed me an explanation, anyway. We were basically strangers, after all.

"You can ask me anything," I offered. "Apparently I love to talk."

He laughed at that. "I'll remember that, if something comes to mind."

The fire was dwindling down. I never did grab the hot dogs. "I can put more logs on the fire if you like," I offered.

Ian glanced down at his watch. "Maybe another time. I have to be up early for work."

"On a Saturday?"

"Yeah," he said. "They're open, so I get scheduled most Saturdays."

"Do you ever get any weekends off?"

"If I ask, I probably could. But I usually just plan around my days off."

I nodded. "Me too. Well, I won't keep you." We both stood and headed back to the house, as it was quicker to the front than going all the way around.

Inside the house, I glanced at him assiduously. "Have a good night." I then approached him and embraced him. He flinched but then wrapped his arms around me. He quickly released me.

He had a small grin spreading from cheek to cheek. "You too, Danyelle."

He turned and let himself out. I was hoping he would have turned around and kissed me. But maybe it was just too soon.

I returned to my bedroom to change back into my sweats. Back in the living room, I lounged under a blanket on the couch and turned on the television for background noise.

Soon a text from Ian crossed my screen. *Thanks for having me over. I had a good time.*

I got all giddy inside. *We should hang out again soon.*

Almost instantly he replied, *I'll text you sometime this week. Good night.*

Sounds good.

I placed the phone to my chest and smiled.

5

Ian kept his promise and invited me out for lunch after a week of back-and-forth texting. At first, the texts were awkward, but then I sent him a funny meme, and he slowly began to exchange random pictures. And this morning he invited me out to lunch.

When we texted, Ian managed small talk. He would engage in everyday conversation and talk about his job or what he was doing at any given moment, but that was it. It wasn't necessarily a bad thing, but still it left me wondering and kept my head spinning, trying to read him and pick up on any of his cues.

But one thing for sure was he had asked to be off from work today, a Saturday, to take me out to lunch.

How about I meet you at one? Ian had texted.

Okay. I sent a smile face emoticon to complete the text.

I hope you are hungry. The food is delicious. But I won't keep you. See you at one. He too responded with a smile face.

Okay, I look forward to it.

I closed out of the messages. Now it was just a waiting game.

When I finally got around to calling Kiera, she wanted all the juicy details, and she wasn't even a little bit sorry that she had put both of us in such an awkward spot. I could picture her smirk, her eyes gleaming in pride.

It didn't stop there, either. She insisted I call her so she could come over before our next date, if one were to call going out for lunch a "date." But she called it a date, and I subconsciously was also calling it a date. She insisted I needed to make an impression.

I bit my lip. Kiera was wrong, and I knew it. I didn't want to tell her Ian figured out *I* wasn't the one who invited him over that night, but it didn't really matter. I assumed Ian wanted me to be myself, but had it paid off? God, I hoped so. This whole thing was entirely awkward, and I couldn't put my finger on why. All I knew were two things: I was hooked on discovering more about Ian, and the small talk wasn't cutting it.

It was almost time for me to leave for lunch. I had put on a clean blouse and a pair of slacks. Ian had worn a shirt and jeans every time I had seen him. Maybe I was overthinking it? Clearly, he wasn't, but then again, wasn't that what guys did anyway? He did arrive shortly after I—Kiera if I was being specific—had interrupted him while he was cooking dinner.

I placed my phone on the coffee table and paced the room. I was jittery. Why was I so nervous? Then my phone pinged, and that little green light blinked. A new message? I played with the collar of my shirt before reaching for it. What if he canceled?

I let out a sigh of relief when I realized it was just a text from Mom. *Hey Sweetie, I heard from a friend of a friend that you met someone special. When do I get to meet him?*

I swore under my breath. How did she find out about Ian? Surely Kiera didn't tell someone, who told someone else, like a game of telephone ending up back at my mother.

I'm not dating anyone yet. I did make a new friend, though. If it becomes something more, I'll let you know.

I hoped the questions would wait, but less than a minute later, she texted me again. *So, your friend is a man, correct?*

Yes. I swirled my finger over the screen as I tried to formulate a response that would hopefully put this conversation to rest, at least temporarily.

I kept checking back at the time. It was just after noon. I needed to think of a response just in case Mom decided to drive by. Before I could, she texted again.

Oh, I just heard that you were getting close to a certain fellow. I kind of hoped you had found someone.

He is a good friend. I'll call you tonight. Love you Mom.

Mom wanted me to meet someone. Big surprise there. But I guessed she also had high expectations, and I didn't think Ian would fit her criteria. She wanted what was best for me, and I felt the pressure of disappointing those high expectations. They were like bullet points on a spreadsheet. It was so meticulous.

I love you, too. Look forward to hearing from you. Dany

I closed out of her message and went back to my homepage. It was time for me to head out.

I sent a quick text to Ian, telling him I was on my way. I was usually early whenever I met anyone. Those who arrive late and try to excuse themselves are just rude, plain and simple. I hoped that Ian wasn't one of those people and that if he did show up late, he didn't try to make an excuse.

Traffic was unexpectedly backed up going over the bridge to the Southwest area of the city. There was an abundance of restaurants, and the locals gave the area the nickname "Food Central." Ian had recommended the little restaurant we were going to. I hadn't eaten there before, but I was open to trying new things. He described this place as casual. "Think early Saturday hangover comfort food," he said. Whatever that meant.

Ian was waiting by the front door of the little diner. He wore a button-up black long-sleeve shirt with a pair of cargo pants. I glanced at him from head to toe. Here I thought a t-shirt and jeans was his every day attire, but I guess it goes to show that he has a classier style.

"Hey," he said when he spotted me. He froze several feet from me and smiled. He reached forward and hugged me briefly.

I made a mental note to make more of an effort to try to expand our conversation beyond small talk. "How are you?"

"I'm good," he replied as he took several strides toward the door. "Shall we go in?"

I nodded. "Yes." I hoped that being in a more intimate (even if it was casual) setting would open up more meaningful conversation.

We were greeted by a middle-aged woman with dyed copper hair and hints of grey at the roots. "For how many?"

Ian glanced at me and quickly answered. "Two."

The lady nodded. "This way, please."

We were seated at a booth by the far end of the restaurant. There were a few others, mainly older people, which I thought was odd, considering that Ian described the place as serving comforting hangover food. I associated young adults with going for some comfort food after a night of drinking. But maybe they just served delicious food.

Once the hostess was a fair distance away, Ian opened up the menu. I followed suit. I was kind of used to a bit of conversation before ordering, but maybe he was just hungry.

I was delighted to see they had baked macaroni and cheese, grilled eggplant, and some wraps. I could understand why he liked this place. I scanned the list of wraps. Chicken Caesar. Nope. Chicken, bacon, ranch. Now, that was up my alley.

Ian glanced up from the menu. "Have you ever tried grilled eggplant?"

"Eggplant yes, grilled eggplant no."

A small grin crossed his face. "Would you like to try some?"

I gnawed at my lip. I wasn't really in the mood for eggplant, but I didn't want to say no. "Sure, I'll try some."

He smirked. "You won't be disappointed."

"What else are you planning on getting?" I asked, trying to engage in some kind of conversation.

"The Breakfast Slammer Burrito."

I glanced down at the menu.

"It's on the next page."

I turned the page to another long list of food delicacies. I scanned the lists until I found the item in question. It consisted of scrambled eggs, bacon, sausage, cheddar cheese, and hollandaise sauce wrapped in a whole wheat, homemade tortilla. That did sound pretty good.

"What about you?" he asked. "What are you getting?"

I turned back to the previous page and pointed at the chicken bacon wrap. "This."

"Good choice." He smiled. "They even make the ranch from scratch."

I licked my lips. Homemade ranch was delicious. I often went for convenience. I didn't like to spend that much time in the kitchen when I could get the same thing already prepared from the store. But I would never turn down ranch dressing, and it even made me extremely excited when it was prepared for me.

He chuckled. "Waylon always orders a side of ranch whenever we come here."

My excitement wavered, and a coolness circled around me. So he took me to the same place he and Waylon went. I don't know what it was, but it seemed like Waylon was his only other friend. He spoke so highly of the man, and he didn't talk about anyone else, not even a mention of anything regarding Alaska. There had to be something good he could talk about.

"So, how often do you come here?" I started.

"I used to come here once or twice a month but haven't been lately. I'm trying to pay off my parking tickets. Just a few more hundred dollars before I can put this behind me."

I shot him a sympathetic glance. I felt a twinge of guilt as he continued to drive without insurance.

"Why do you keep risking getting caught driving, when you could just ask for me to come pick you up?" He drove a lot. Many times over the last week, he had driven from one place or another. I understood the necessity to drive to and from work, but to drive out to eat, to my house, or just at his leisure, seemed risky.

"I try to be careful." His voice was quiet, almost inaudible.

"I just don't want you to get pulled over. It isn't a dig at you, I promise."

He smiled. "I appreciate the concern."

I closed the menu and took a deep breath. There had been something that had been bothering me. "Can I ask you something?"

"Yes?" He looked nervous. "What is it?"

"How much did you spend out of pocket because of our accident?

He brushed his hand through his hair. "It doesn't matter. I just needed to make sure things were right. Like I said, another month or two, and everything will be back to normal."

"How much do you owe in tickets?" I pressed.

"Just a few hundred dollars, like I said." He turned to search the room for the waitress.

"It was my fault for crashing into you. Let me help you by paying off the rest of your tickets so you don't keep driving illegally." I offered softly. If he had insurance, I would be out more money than I was offering, and my premiums would go up.

"No," he said firmly as the waitress finally approached us.

"Can I take your order?"

Ian listed off what he wanted in a flat, calculated voice. I had ticked him off, when all I wanted to do was make things right.

"How about a side job?" I quickly remembered the leaky tap in the kitchen.

He jumped. "Side job? Doing what?"

"I have a leaky faucet. You need money and I need a plumber, so it's a win-win. What do you say?"

He gritted his teeth. "I'm sure it'd be an easy fix. I know what you are doing. I appreciate it, but I need to cover my own bills. Don't worry. I've been through much worse. Much, much worse . . ." His voice trailed off and he avoided eye contact with me. "My father always told me that we don't accept handouts from people."

I felt the urge to question his line of thinking but decided to stop myself. Especially since he told me Waylon helped him out when he came to town.

"How about we do something fun after lunch?" I changed the subject. I wasn't going to get much out of him like I wanted, so maybe I could learn a bit more about his interests.

"What did you have in mind?"

"Movie, bowling? What do you want to do?"

He perked up at that. "Bowling? I haven't been in a while."

I raised an eyebrow. "Do you like bowling?"

He snickered. "When I get all the pins down, sure."

I laughed at that. "I'm pretty sure everyone likes it when they have a strike."

The waitress returned with our food. The chicken wrap arrived on a rectangular white plate. It was neatly wrapped, and I could see pieces of grilled chicken and crisp green lettuce drizzled with that much-anticipated ranch poking out. It looked so scrumptious, I couldn't wait to bite into it. Ian had failed to mention that this place was on the higher end of casual. He drummed his fingers on the table when she plopped the plate of grilled eggplant in front of him. They were thinly sliced with perfect grilled marks.

"Here." He held up the plate, and I reluctantly grabbed myself a slice. "You'll love it, I promise."

I took a bite. It tasted okay, slightly crunchy with a hint of Cajun spice. But I still wasn't in the mood for it. I smiled at him and replied, "It's delicious."

"See?"

I grinned. "Yeah, it's good alright. Thanks."

Then I glanced down at my wrap, which I was actually excited for. I took a bite, my mouth on the tip of watering. I was in awe. Ian wasn't joking; the ranch was delightful, to die for.

"Again, what did I tell you?" Ian said.

"You weren't lying. This is delicious."

Ian seemed to take some pride in being right. Not in a self-righteous kind of way, but in a people-pleaser way. I hadn't known him that long, so my assumptions could be way off.

Ian pulled out his phone, stared, and frowned for a moment before turning his focus back on me. "I'm glad you like it."

"Something wrong?" I noted his left leg bounced under the table.

"It's just work. They are understaffed, and they needed me today. They had a few emergency calls. One for a burst pipe. I just feel guilty for saying no."

"It's not your problem," I said. "It's up to them to hire enough employees so you can enjoy your day off. It's not like you take Saturdays off often."

"There is a shortage of qualified people."

I shrugged. "Again, not your problem."

"I guess."

I felt my throat constrict. I was annoyed, and I couldn't help it. He and I were supposed to be enjoying hanging out, but it seemed like he'd rather go to work. I ate in silence, trying not to let my annoyance show.

"I'm not going to work, if that is what you're upset about."

I forced a smile. "I'm not upset." I took a deep breath, deciding to capitalize on this moment. "I just didn't want you to go. I enjoy your company."

"Oh?"

I probed further. "What do you say to that?"

He blushed a deep crimson. "I enjoy you, too." I hoped he wasn't agreeing with me just for the sake of it.

"I just don't get out much. I don't date or hang out with men often." I found the words slipping out of my mouth. "I'm a homebody who watches history documentaries and sews."

"There is nothing wrong with history."

I sighed, somewhat disappointed, as I expected a different response. "Do you watch history documentaries?" I inquired. Normally, I'd be at the edge of my seat, excited to talk, but I felt kind of sad and didn't know why.

"I was interested in medieval history in high school."

A glimpse of hope emerged. My love of history was a big part of who I was. I didn't expect him or anyone to enjoy it as much as me, but to possibly have the openness to discuss it made a huge impact.

"Maybe instead of bowling, I can teach you how to change a tire, and then we can watch a documentary," Ian suggested.

"So is this like a . . ." I stopped myself. "Sounds good."

"What were you going to say?" he asked.

"It was nothing."

He didn't seem convinced but didn't say anything.

"Let's just finish eating."

He nodded.

We ate in silence for a few minutes, when mid-bite, Ian put his fork down and looked behind me. I turned my head to see Waylon.

Waylon said a few words to the hostess and ambled toward our table.

"I thought I'd find you here, Ian." He then turned to me. "It's good to see you again, Danyelle."

"What's up?" Ian asked.

Waylon placed his hand on the table, inches from Ian. "When you are done eating, I need you to stop by the shop," he said curtly, and then he turned and walked out the front door.

"What was that?" I asked.

Ian gnawed at his upper lip. "I don't know, but it seemed serious."

I didn't show my disappointment. "Then maybe you should go." I couldn't help but wonder why Waylon hadn't just texted him.

"Yeah, I probably should," he mumbled. "I'm sorry."

I reached over and touched his hand. "We can do it next time."

He nodded. "I really didn't know he was going to show up."

"It's fine," I whispered. "Maybe we can hang out later tonight, if you're not too tired."

"I'm glad you understand."

I felt like I didn't have a choice. He didn't know me well, and Waylon was his friend, so I understood that he would get priority over me.

After we finished eating, we paid and headed outside.

Ian hugged me once more. "I'll text you later, I promise," he said.

"Have a good afternoon." I smiled.

He reached in as if he was going to kiss me, but he stopped and backed up a few steps. "You as well." He gave a little wave and then walked off.

6

I watched my last client pull away. She had just picked up the corset I had designed and sewed. It had originally been part of a larger concept for the sort of Victorian gown worn by women in the 1800s, but halfway through the project, my client decided she only wanted the corset. She claimed she had a different vision, but I was convinced that she just didn't want to pay the price I was charging for the full outfit. It was frustrating, because I didn't like to have an unfinished look, but I also couldn't work for free.

I cleaned up my workspace, retreated to my bedroom, and sunk into my bed. I refused to continue to let it occupy my mind. I took out my phone and saw that I had a few missed texts. One was from Mom.

Are you up for some shopping tomorrow?

Tomorrow was Saturday, and I hadn't confirmed any plans with Ian.

Sure, I replied. *Is Saoirse coming as well?* A few months ago, my cousin went to stay with Mom while my aunt was having surgery. She was fourteen — sweet at times, but incredibly entitled. I found myself having to bite my tongue.

No, she is going out with friends, so we'll have some one-on-one time.

I look forward to it.

I had another text from Kiera.

So . . . How are you and Ian doing!!?? I half laughed and sighed.

All right. We hung out a few times. Hoping to hang out with him this weekend.

Oh? She replied.

Yeah, he's a nice guy but not very open. I feel like I have to drag information out of him.

At first, he was open with me, telling me about the parking tickets. But now it was like pulling teeth to get him to tell me anything. He brought up Alaska but then shut down. Not to mention the weird dynamic between him and Waylon. How long had they known one another?

Some people aren't as open about their life as you are, Hun. Just enjoy his company and he will probably come around when he's ready.

I knew she was right, even if it wasn't the response I wanted to hear. I wanted her to validate my feelings that he should be more open. I guess my expectations were too high. We only met and started hanging out a few weeks ago, even though it felt longer. Maybe he was still trying to feel me out.

I know.

Why don't you go text him right now and set up a date? Go hang out, have fun, and loosen up.

I so badly wanted to tell her that we weren't dating. We hugged, went out to lunch, and I invited him over.

Okay, I replied.

I hadn't talked to Ian since last night, so maybe he was up to hang out for a bit, even if it was tomorrow afternoon.

As I scrolled through messages, I was surprised to see he had sent me a message this morning, and either I was too tired to remember or someone else read my messages, which was unlikely.

Hey, how you doing? he had texted.

Sorry for the long delay. It's been a busy day. Just finished a corset for a client.

It's fine, he texted back, quickly followed by: *I was just going to go get some coffee. Join me?*

Sure, I'll meet you there.

I wasted no time leaving. I was halfway to the café when I realized I hadn't changed my clothes. *Oh well,* I thought to myself. Usually I cared and tried to look put together, but I guess Ian would get a glimpse of my tank top, hoodie, and sweatpants look—also known as lounging- around-the-house wear.

As I got out of the car, I noticed Ian waiting by his. He approached my car and hugged me. "It's good to see you."

I smiled as a warm fluttering feeling flowed through me. "Me too."

As we made our way to the café, Ian and I walked closer than we ever did before. Kiera was right. I needed to loosen up and go with the flow. It was obvious, at least from today, that he was warming up to me. Maybe that would mean there was a possibly of something more.

I ordered my usual green tea with cream and he ordered a black coffee with two creams and one sugar. Before I could pay, he placed a bill on the counter telling the cashier to keep the change. I glanced at him and he smiled.

"You're a little brat," I whispered as we walked to our table.

He chuckled and we sat down across from one another. "How's work?"

I shrugged. "I had a half-day then had to finish an order for a client."

"What exactly do you do?" he asked as he looked attentively into my eyes.

I had mentioned a few times that I designed costumes, but I had never gone into detail. "Well, I design and sew a lot of costumes for parties. I'm also a seamstress. It provides a lot of my income, but it's not always steady, so I also work at the gift shop, which is very flexible."

He tapped his fingers lightly on the table and took a sip. "Hmm. If you could make one costume right now for any time period, what would it be?"

I put my chin on my hand and my elbow to table. I had some preferences for time periods, but not a definite favorite. "I'd like to make a Marie Antoinette inspired gown. I could just picture all the silks and lace and shifts. Oh, and the form fitting corsets. Marie Antoinette was so fashionable. "

He stared at me as if I had grown a second head. "Who?"

"Marie Antoinette? You know, the queen of France, who was executed for treason back in the seventeen hundreds?"

He took another swig of his beverage. "And why would you want to make a gown based on someone like that?"

I was shocked. "Inspiration. She may not have been a very nice person, but she was very fashionable." Deep down, I just really liked to make nice clothes.

He nodded. "I see."

I grinned. "I have a few pieces I designed that are a modern take on medieval wear for men." I remembered that he liked the medieval ages in high school. If he offered, he could be my muse.

Ian fiddled with the napkin holder. "Now, that I have to see."

"I could show you."

"Okay, show me," he said forcefully.

"Right now?" I inquired, hoping he was serious.

He nodded and quickly chugged the rest of his beverage. "Yes."

He stood up. I stood up too and grabbed my half-full, still hot cup of tea. He led the way into the parking lot. Who was this, and where did they take Ian? Just last time, he was so timid, shy, and awkward as hell. Maybe he was overthinking everything like I was, and maybe he thought he needed to be less shy and more open.

"Are you coming?" Ian asked.

I realized I was standing in the middle of the parking lot, gazing at God knows what. "Yeah." I responded, rather frazzled. "I am coming." I needed to get my nerves under control. This was a good thing.

I sped walked the rest of the way to my car, my face burning.

"I'll meet you there, okay?"

"Okay."

I followed Ian out of the parking lot, toward my house. It was kind of surreal that he was leading me. My impression of him was he was a follower. It was good to see this side of him.

He pulled up in front of my house as I pulled into my driveway. He didn't exit his Honda until I exited my own car. He slowly, almost mechanically, strolled up the driveway behind me.

"I'm still amazed you own," he muttered.

I stood akimbo. "Why? Have you ever considered buying?"

Ian glanced downward and shook his head. "No, I haven't. Not a fan of debt."

I nodded as I opened the front door. "A mortgage isn't a bad thing. It ends up being cheaper then rent. At least it was for me."

Ian stood in the doorway tensely. "I just don't like having debt. I don't care what it is." He looked away then back at me. "Sorry, I just do things a certain way."

He didn't say anything else until we got into the living room. I didn't respond because he seemed tense. That was the last thing I wanted. Remembering Kiera's advice, I decided I'd go with the flow.

"Make yourself at home."

He sat down. "Thanks."

"So, what do you usually do in your spare time?" I realized I brought him here originally to show him my fashion, but I was still hoping to learn a little more about him. Surely there was something he'd share with me.

He leaned forward so his elbows were on his knees. "I tinker a lot."

"Tinker? With what?" When I thought about tinkering, I thought about a man covered in grease, tinkering underneath a car propped up on a jack.

"With pretty much anything. I like to take apart things and put them back together. It's relaxing."

"That's cool. So, I take it you're pretty handy."

Ian laughed. "I like to think so."

I crossed my legs, sitting on the sofa a foot away from him. "I have my own set of skills as well. I can hem a pair of pants or sew on a button. Heck, I could make an entire wardrobe for any time period if time permitted."

"And you were going to show me some of your work."

I stood straight up. "Oh yeah." I hadn't forgotten, but I was thrilled he remembered. "Come, I'll show you."

I didn't wait for a response before I headed out of the living room for the stairs. "This is my bedroom," I said as I pointed at the master, before I reached the adjacent room. "And the bathroom is at the end of the hall on your left, if you need it."

"Okay."

I opened the door to my sewing room. A large wooden desk I inherited from my grandmother held my sewing machine. My parents bought it for me for my twenty-fifth birthday and it was top of the line. On each side of the room were hangers with designs, some for clients, some I planned to take to trade shows to sell, and some for me.

Ian's mouth opened as he ran his hand along the sleeve of an unfinished long-sleeve early 20th century dress. "You made all this?"

I retrieved one of the medieval inspired looks I promised to show him. "This is my modern version of a woolen tunic, which was commonly worn by men in the medieval times." I held up an oversized, white cotton tunic, with a belt, and a pair of leather pants. "Instead of wool, I used thin cotton. But the shape is very similar."

"It looks nice."

I smirked. "How about you do something for me?"

He raised an eyebrow. "What?"

"Would you try it on? I haven't had anyone actually try it on."

Ian took a step back. "I don't know." He looked away.

I was slightly disappointed. "It's okay. But you would still look sexy as hell in it."

Ian laughed nervously. "It isn't that. I—I just don't want my picture taken."

"Who says I was going to take a picture?" Speaking of pictures, why was taking a picture a bad thing? But I reminded myself to remain open. "I just wanted to see what it looked like on a male's body."

Ian breathed an exhale of relief. "Okay, if you want, I'll try it on."

Without a second thought, Ian took off his shirt. He had a six pack and well defined biceps, which I had seen a hint of when we met. I stared at his chest and then back at his face. He grew a deep red.

I took the tunic off its hanger and handed it to him.

He took it, his arm trembling as he put it on. I helped him with the belt without saying a word. I pointed to the wall-sized mirror.

"What do you think?" I asked. "Because I like it."

"It's interesting," Ian admitted. "It kind of has a wearable art feel to it."

"I think so too." When I designed it, I wanted to combine medieval fashion with a very artistic but wearable silhouette. "It really goes well with anything. But I chose leather because I felt it gave it an edge."

"I like it," Ian said.

I blushed as he took it off, and I put it back on the hanger. "Thanks for trying it on. It really brought my vision to light."

Grinning, Ian pulled me to his chest. I wrapped my arms around his muscular body as his warm breath spread down my neck. I shivered with need as my body tensed. My breath hitched, halted as we naturally parted. "Hopefully you don't have to go home too soon," I said. I remembered back to the campfire and how around this time, he had gotten up and left because he had to work the next day. I hoped he'd stay a bit longer this time.

"I could stay a little longer. I don't have to go home quite yet," Ian replied.

"How about a movie?" I suggested. It seemed like an innocent suggestion. It didn't require much talking, yet it would be nice to just enjoy his company.

"All right."

Those words were like music to my ears, and it would make up for when he ditched me at lunch for whatever Waylon wanted. I still found that incredibly odd, but I hadn't thought to ask what he'd wanted. It'd probably be met with some huge resistance.

Once we were back in the living room, he sat on the couch. I retrieved the television remote and handed it to him. "Here. Pick a movie or television show. I'll be right back." I was hoping he'd pick something he was interested in so I could learn a bit more about him.

I headed into the kitchen. I couldn't watch a movie without popcorn or drinks. Dots of perspiration dotted my forehead.

I took several shallow breaths as I opened up the fridge. I didn't even know what he liked to drink besides coffee. I had some water and soda. So maybe I'd just bring a couple of each. I had barbeque and plain chips in the cupboard. I guess I'd just give him an option. I swallowed hard again. Here goes nothing. I retrieved the snacks and made my way back to the living room.

Ian sat the remote back on the coffee table, and leaned back into the couch cushion, still in a semi-seated position.

I set the snacks on the table. "I'm not sure what you like, so I brought a few options. Help yourself."

Ian reached over and grabbed a bottle of water, which wasn't surprising considering his physique. I grabbed myself a soda and cracked it open, then reached over for my other remote that controlled the lights. I dimmed them.

Ian beamed.

"Who wants a glare on a television?" I said and smiled back. "So, what did you choose?"

"It's a show called The Other Boleyn Girl. Sounds like something you'd like."

I smiled. He was really paying attention when I said I liked history. I reached over and gave him a quick hug and plopped down beside him.

Soon the only sound in the room was chips crunching. Ian's gaze seemed to wander, and I couldn't focus either, even if it was a show I enjoyed. I inched my hand over toward his and lightly brushed my finger along his open palm. He flinched but didn't pull away. Instead he grabbed my hand and held it.

I tingled on the inside. I scooched over so we were nearly touching. Ian's leg trembled a bit, so I pulled away. *Too soon?* I hoped I didn't make him instantly uncomfortable, especially when today had been going so well.

He did a one-eighty — literally — and pulled me gently back toward him. He snuggled my head into the crease of his upper arm. Where did this sudden vulnerability come from? His warm flesh brought a sense of security, much like I was wrapped tightly in a cocoon. I almost felt like I was imagining it.

We didn't say anything, as the television noise became background noise, and my mind floated. Ian was a good cuddler. Maybe I could get past him being a bit closed off emotionally. He was pretty open in other areas. He'd be a perfect muse for my fashion. He had a great body, after all. Then he could show me some handy things, like changing a tire, or how to change a light bulb. Okay, I did that already, but I could see what he could bring to the table.

His breathing became labored. I carefully glanced upward. His eyes were closed. I didn't want him to wake up, and I certainly didn't want him to move. So, I closed my eyes again. I wasn't one to lie in one position for long, so eventually I would wake up and need to move, and he'd wake up and probably leave for home. It seemed like a slightly selfish but innocent plan. I figured if he didn't want to be here or was uncomfortable, he would have made any excuse to leave.

I closed my eyes and drifted off to sleep.

The following morning, I was awakened by pounding on my door. Ian and I both jumped. It was light out. Ian was as pale as a ghost and hurried to pull his shirt over his head. I guess he never had put his shirt back on from yesterday. I got up and looked out the window.

It was my *mother*.

"Oh, shit," I mumbled.

"Who is it?"

"My mom." I sighed. "I haven't told her about you, us, or whatever this is."

Ian took a deep breath and exhaled a sigh of relief.

"What did you think?" I asked.

"I'm not sure." He quickly reached for his phone. "I better get going. I have to go to work soon."

"Sorry," I mumbled. "But she is coming up here, and she is going to talk to you. There is no way around it."

"Does she normally come by so early?"

"What time is it?"

He glanced at his phone. "Seven forty-five."

I shook my head. "No. She's just nosey."

Then the doorbell rang.

"I better get that." I went to answer the door with Ian following closely behind.

"It's about time you answered the . . ." She stopped mid-sentence. "Why, Dany, I had no idea you had company."

I stared at her with that *don't bullshit me* look. The only reason she was here before eight on a weekend, especially on the day we were hanging out, was because she saw his car and was curious.

"This is Ian," I quickly introduced him. "Ian, this is my mom."

"It's nice to meet you," Mom said quickly as she extended her hand. Ian took it and smiled.

"It's nice to meet you as well," he said with ease. So maybe he had experience with meeting the parents before. Interesting.

"Well, aren't you a gentleman?" Mom grinned.

"Well, thank you ma'am."

Mom looked at me and winked and turned back to him. "Now, call me Sharla. None of this ma'am business. I'm not *that* old."

Ian bit his lip. "Okay, Ma- Sharla."

"Don't you have a meeting to get to?" I asked Ian, attempting to save him from the questioning I knew was coming.

"Meeting?" Ian looked at me, confused.

"With your boss?" I hated mentioning work because I knew Mom would instantly ask about it.

"Oh? What do you do, Ian?"

"I'm a plumber. And yes, I do have a meeting at eight thirty, and I need to go home and change. I really hate to leave so suddenly."

"Oh, I won't keep you, lad. You have a wonderful day."

Ian didn't even stay long enough to give me a hug. He just quickly squeezed his way out between us. My mother even watched him go.

I turned my focus to her.

"Why are you here so early?" I knew, but I was kind of annoyed and disappointed that she had interrupted an intimate moment.

"I was in the area and saw the car out front."

"It could have been anyone's car."

"Tell me about him. I thought you weren't dating anyone."

I sighed as I strode back into the house with Mom closely behind. "I'm not even sure if we are dating yet. We were hanging out and fell asleep in the living room. Nothing else happened."

"Well, he seemed like a really nice lad."

"He is really nice and responsible, too." I slipped a little lie in there. I didn't want to tell her he didn't have a license.

"Where did you two meet?"

"At the body shop," I laughed. "He was getting his car fixed at the same time."

"I see," she said again.

I stood. "I'm going to get dressed, then we can hit an early breakfast. How does that sound?"

"Okay."

I scurried up to my room where I planted face first into the bed with my phone in hand.

Sorry about the interruption. I had a good night last night. I hope you have a good day.

I thought about how he had slept the night with me, shirtless. I wondered where this was going and really hoped it was leading to something more. I really did like him and it was evident he liked me too.

7

Come over.

I hovered over that text before sending it. What was I thinking? And what were we supposed to do when he got here? I couldn't stop thinking about him and how I had felt waking up next to him, even though nothing had happened. But it could have happened. I was lonely, and Kiera was right that I had been single for way too long and Ian may be the escape I needed from reality. There was just something about him that made me want more.

It was Saturday afternoon and he should just be leaving work. I knew he wasn't working the following day, and I hoped he'd stay the night again. I wasn't sure if the last time was a fluke or if he had really wanted to stay with me.

All right. I'm going to go home real quick and change, and then I'll be right over.

I smiled as I pictured him shirtless, sprawled out on my couch. *Sounds good, see you soon.* I found myself shifting on the couch, and my stomach stirred with flutters of butterflies. Every time he texted me, a smile from cheek to cheek lit up my face, and the moments between spending time with one another felt like an eternity. I wished I could see him more than once or twice a week, but I was afraid to suggest more because I wasn't even sure if we were just friends or something more.

Either way, I needed to do something, because I couldn't deny my feelings. Ian captivated me, and when he left, I felt so alone.

I sent a quick text to Kiera. *Guess who is coming over again? Someone really likes you. Xo xo xo*

I blushed. I was sure I liked Ian a little more than he liked me. I doubt he thought about me as much as I did him. Maybe it was a guy thing. I never really dated much. But then I remembered the lunch date and my mom's rude interruption. Even after all that, he wanted to spend time with me. That had to mean he enjoyed my company, right?

Kiera responded, interrupting my floundering. *Just remember not to push too much for him to open up. Flirt a lot and keep things light.*

I smirked. *Noted. Text later.*

Ian did respond better to casual talking. So far, not bombarding him with questions had loosened him up. He smiled more and laughed more. So maybe that was the key to his vulnerability. I wanted him to trust me and feel comfortable around me. Maybe if he felt that, he would open up.

The doorbell yanked me out of my floundering thoughts. I hurried with a skip and a jump to the front door. Ian and I smiled at the same time when I opened the door. He gave me an extended hug and rubbed the back of my neck before reluctantly letting go.

"How are you?" he asked.

"Good," I said. My face grew hot. I don't know why I was blushing, but I was. "Sit down?"

He nodded, and we both sat for just a moment before he asked, "Do you like wine?"

I jumped but nodded. "The odd glass, yeah."

"I have a bottle of Moscato in my car that my boss was giving out after some house party, if you'd like some."

In the back of my mind, I knew it was probably not a good idea, but a couple of glasses of wine could loosen us both up.

And surely, he wouldn't drink and drive, so he would probably stay the night.

I shrugged, trying to keep things casual and calm, when really, I wanted to make out with him. What the hell was wrong with me? "Sure."

He rose. "I'll go grab it real quick." Before I could object, he ambled for the door.

I sat there, reprimanding myself. I shouldn't be drinking. Did I already forget what happened last time? I don't know what had gotten into me that night. I drank so much, I woke up the next day not remembering where I was or how I had gotten got there. I was positive I'd had sex, but I didn't remember consenting or anything. I shook my head. I was a good girl. I needed to keep it together and not repeat that mistake. But I didn't think Ian would take advantage. He had been respectful of me so far.

Ian let himself back in with the promised wine in hand.

"Let me get some glasses."

I stood up, and Ian pulled me in for a kiss. It lingered for a minute before he let me go. Shocked for a moment, I burst into a grin. I was speechless as I turned to make my way to the kitchen. I couldn't stop smiling. It was like he'd read my mind. Where had this new, spontaneous Ian come from? I kind of liked it. I retrieved the glasses and returned to the living room.

He took them from me. "Here, let me help you." He poured two glasses and handed one to me. "I'm not sure how this will taste, but here goes!"

I laughed as I took a sip. It didn't taste bad. "It's a little sweet. It doesn't taste quite like my usual."

Ian finished off the glass quickly. "The only way I'd finish it. I think next time I'll stick to beer."

So, he was a beer guy. That was good to know.

"I prefer a simple glass of red wine." I wanted to keep the conversation going. Keep him comfortable and sharing more about himself.

"Yeah."

There was the small talk again. I bounced my knee. I could act so many ways, but I was worried about being inappropriate, especially if we were just friends.

"Is something wrong?" Ian finally asked.

"I—I..." I stuttered. "What are we?" I started but stopped.

Ian raised an eyebrow as he reached for the wine bottle. "What do you mean?"

I felt my face get hot. "Are we just friends, or are we, you know . . . ?"

A slow smile emerged on his face. "Dating?" It was more like a statement then a question. "I mean, we kind of are. I like you."

"I like you, too."

Ian rubbed the back of his neck. "Do you want to date me?"

I bit my upper lip. "Yeah, I do." I glanced downward before forcing eye contact. "We've been seeing each other for over a month. I think we get along. I was just hoping for . . . something more."

Then Ian smiled while bouncing his left leg. "You're not like any other girl I have met. I'd love to get to know you better."

I beamed, a warmth radiating from within me. I reached over and kissed him. I couldn't wait to tell Kiera I was now officially dating a sexy, handsome hunk. "Well, that settles that. Shall we drink to that?"

Ian poured himself a bit of wine to match the amount still in my glass. "Okay, just a little, because to be honest, this tastes like shit."

I laughed and we clicked glasses. I finished my glass and set it on the coffee table. Ian did the same. "How about we order some takeout? I'm hungry and lazy."

"Okay. What do you like?" Ian asked.

"Pizza?" Everyone liked pizza. It was a safe choice.

"Sounds good to me."

I wanted to sigh. I had hoped he would suggest what kind. But he didn't, and I wasn't aware of his preferences yet. "What kind of pizza do you like?" I wasn't overly picky, but I liked more than just simply cheese.

"Anything is fine."

I nodded and proceeded to call the pizza place and order an all-meat pizza for delivery.

"So how was work today?" I asked casually. I inched closer to him.

He shrugged. "The same as any other day."

I nodded. "No overbearing homeowner or barking dogs?"

Ian reached for his glass and the bottle. "I have had my fair share of yippy Chihuahuas who think they are hundred-pound beasts in a four-pound body." He poured himself a glass and filled up mine. "After a while, I learned to block it all out. I do my eight hours, go home and relax, and do it all again the next day."

I bit my lip. Eight hours was like a third of your day. Surely, he would want to have as much fun as he could. At least for me, I tried to talk to as many customers as I could or observe as much as I could. I had stories to tell. But of course, I wasn't him.

Ian glanced at me. "Okay, there was a certain client who lived in an old house, and she had asked me to fix a leaky faucet. I turned her down, but I might just fix it because she asked me to."

I smiled.

I reached for my glass and took a swig. Setting it down, I reached over for Ian's hand. I caressed it while staring right in his eyes. The corners of his mouth turned upward.

I leaned in, our noses touched, and I kissed him. The third kiss of the night. We were on a roll. He wrapped his arms around me as we fell back on the couch. My tongue darted around his lips, and a surge of warmth rushed through me. My body yearned for him. It closed the distance between us. His lips parted and I accessed. He tasted fruity and I loved every minute of it. Then we released and stared intensely at one another. No words were needed. Not even a smile. I panted, wanting more.

Then the doorbell rang. Curses. Rain check. First, we eat.

Ian helped me up from the couch and followed me to the door. Before I could hand my credit card to the delivery driver, Ian pulled out his wallet and paid for the pizza.

"Brat!" I teased him.

"You can grab it next time."

I sat on the couch. He plopped down next to me, his thigh touching mine. We ate in silence. He gently placed one hand on my thigh.

I ate slowly while I admired Ian. The contours of his toned abs pressed up against his thin shirt. For a plumber, he was incredibly fit. I really wanted to rip his shirt off and do all sorts of things with him. Our eyes locked. He set down the slice of pizza he was holding, reached over, and kissed me. I pushed his head closer to mine, our lips touched, and the passionate embraces began again. He seized my mouth keenly, our dinner long forgotten. Gone was the coy kiss of earlier, replaced with something urgent and desperate. I almost felt like I'd float away if he let go.

I found my fingers lifting the hem of his shirt. I pulled it over his head. Ian grinned and his fingers went to work, fiddling to unfasten each button on my blouse. It slid down around my slender shoulders and off the couch. I pulled back slightly, unbuttoning my bra and stripping it away.

Our lips met again as his hand brushed over my breast. I gasped.

"Did I do something wrong?" Ian asked. His voice was gruff, but racy as well. I wanted more.

"No," I responded, as I took his hand tenderly and pressed it on my chest, "You're doing everything right."

He shimmied out of his jeans, kicking them away, and went for my skirt, slowly sliding it down over my hips. With a quick yank, my panties were gone.

I gasped at the size of his penis.

He frowned, "What?"

I glared intently into his eyes, pressing a hand to his chest. "I need you."

He leaned over and kissed me, his hand lifting my leg as I allowed him entry. The moment he entered, waves of pleasure charged through me. He trailed kisses from my ear to my collar and back again. I moved against him, with him. Ian breathed heavily with each thrust. Slow. In and out. Until I felt a release. I moaned loudly and tensed before our eyes met.

"Don't stop," I said, through hard, labored breaths, "Keep going."

He responded with a kiss, wrapped around me, and picked up his pace. I moaned his name and released again. He finished soon after. I felt a little sad when he pulled out. I lay on top of him, resting my head on his chest. His heartbeat thumped loudly. I glanced up at him. Beads of sweat drenched his forehead. A smile crossed his face from cheek to cheek as his eyes closed. We didn't say anything else as he held me close.

Soon Ian's breathing softened, and he snorted softly. I lay my head on his chest as it raised up and down. He was so relaxed, so tranquil. But I was awake and alert, and I felt my anxiety raising. The sex was amazing. I enjoyed every damn moment of it. Ian enjoyed it; I know he did. Maybe this was the first step to him opening up to me. That had to mean that he felt safe around me, right?

I shifted a little to find a more comfortable position. Ian grunted but didn't wake. I lay my head back on his chest. I didn't want to wake him up, so I lay there, thinking. My mind spun around and around. My stomach fluttered, remembering the night before and the way he had made me feel.

Then it hit me like a ton of bricks.

Ian and I hadn't used protection.

No, no, no! How could I be so stupid! I lifted my head to Ian sleeping so peacefully. Did he even realize what we had done? It was just a month ago when I had a pregnancy scare, and here I am, making the same mistake over again. I blamed the alcohol. I let my guard down again.

I had to catch my breath.

I tried to talk myself out of it, telling myself I'd go get Plan B. It'd be all right. In the morning I'd talk to Ian about wearing condoms or whatever. I just didn't want a repeat of that night again. My leg trembled. I couldn't help it. I thought I had worked through it, accepted I had blamed it on the alcohol, but that hollow feeling returned.

I couldn't remember what happened that New Year's night. I woke up feeling off. The possibility that my drink was spiked had crossed my mind and I dismissed it. But tonight, I had no excuse. I remembered every moment.

Ian was great. We were now a couple and I wanted this. So why was I ruining this? I wanted to scream. I wanted to tell my stupid brain to stop thinking and let me sleep.

But I couldn't help it. The uncontrollable shivering started. I tried to remain still, but Ian unexpectedly woke up.

He sat right up. "What time is it?" he asked, then stared at me. He frowned. "Are you all right?"

I nodded. "Yeah, I'm just really cold. Would you like to move to my bed?" I glanced at him, hoping and praying he would agree and not insist on going home.

Ian didn't say anything at first.

I forced a smile. "You are just really warm, and..."

He reached over and embraced me. "Okay," he replied.

We got up off the couch, leaving our clothes in a heap on the floor, and traveled upstairs to the bedroom. My bed was comfy, and I hoped lying there with Ian would help with some of the anxiety coursing through my veins a mile a minute.

I got into bed and he stood at the foot.

"I'll be right back. Need to use the bathroom."

"Okay, there is toilet paper under the sink, if you need some."

Ian walked over to me and kissed me. "Okay, be back in a minute."

I smiled. I felt a little better.

A few minutes later he returned and crawled in the bed beside me.

Once we were settled under the blankets, we cuddled.

"Are you sure you're all right?" Ian asked. "Did I do something wrong?"

"No," I said, my hand on his chest. "You were great. It's just . . ." I trailed off.

"Are you sure? It's just you were shaking really badly. Did you have a nightmare?"

I wasn't planning on telling Ian about the pregnancy scare but I didn't want to lie to him. "Ian, I have to tell you something."

He searched my face, apprehensive, but said nothing.

"Here goes nothing." I inhaled sharply. "The day we met, I was driving back from the doctor's office. I had a pregnancy scare. I just realized we didn't take extra precautions, so I'm a bit freaked out, that's all."

Ian puckered his brow. "Sorry, I never expected for this to happen. I'll be sure to bring some condoms for next time."

I rested my head down on him. "Thanks for understanding."

He kissed me on the forehead. "Goodnight."

"Night," I whispered.

I wanted to tell him about the New Year's Party, and how I didn't remember what happened, but it was too soon. But I knew I needed to tell someone, because I wasn't okay. I kept making foolish decisions, and my anxiety was at an all-time high. I didn't want to ruin this relationship before it had a chance to take off. Maybe it was time to confide in Kiera. I didn't know who else to talk to.

8

Ian spent the night nearly every day this week and I couldn't be happier. I sat on the couch as he came from upstairs, fully dressed. It was barely noon on a Saturday. He had started asking his work for Saturdays off, and he had gotten two out of the last three he requested. I hid a grimace. What I really wanted was to crawl back in bed and cuddle or watch television. He didn't say he had anywhere to be.

He sat beside me. "You look good this morning." He reached over and kissed me gently on the forehead.

I raised an eyebrow and kissed him back. "I don't look good. I look like I just rolled out of bed. Quite literally." I had unkempt hair and was wearing an oversized sweater I "borrowed" from Ian and a pair of loose silk shorts with big flowers on them.

"You are still beautiful."

I smiled and embraced him. Even though I didn't feel it, it felt good to be complimented. "So what's the plan? Should I get dressed?" Here I was, hoping he had somewhere in mind.

"No," he said and stood. "But I am going out to run a quick errand."

"Where?"

"Surprise," he said.

I frowned. "You know I don't like surprises."

Ian smiled and let out a long, drawn-out sigh. "Fine, I'll give you a little hint."

I sighed in just as an exaggerated way as he had. "Okay."

"I'm going to make us a delicious lunch. This time, I'm bringing cuisine to you."

That piqued my interest. Ian did have a decent palate for food, and I had no doubt he'd bring home something delicious. But still, I didn't like being in suspense. "Hurry, hurry. Don't keep me waiting. Time's a tickin'."

Ian smirked. "Someone's bossy."

I gave him a dirty, playful look. "Brat!"

Ian laughed as he stood. "I'll be back soon, I promise. Love you."

"Love you, too."

I watched as he ambled for the front door, shutting it softly behind him. Once he was gone, my thoughts turned to what he was going to make. What did Ian Fogg have up his sleeve? Maybe he'd make me an Alaskan dish from his childhood. I shook my head. That was unlikely. My guess was he was going to buy some eggplant. He bragged—not in an arrogant way, because Ian wasn't arrogant—of the many different ways he could eat, prepare, or enjoy it.

I paced. Maybe I should go out and grab some wine. But what if Ian came back before I returned? Besides, it was a Saturday morning. By the time we ate, it would be an early lunch. Maybe I should have insisted on going with him. I hated surprises, after all.

I heard my door bell ring just then, and the front door opened before I could stand. Kiera stood, leaning halfway against the door, then closed it behind her. "Hey girl!"

"Um, hi," I said apprehensively. "What's up?"

She ambled in a tank top and tight pair of jeans. "You didn't return my texts, so I thought I'd stop by."

I sat straight up. "Oh, shoot. My phone is in the bedroom. Sorry, I was busy." I winked. Ian and I were a little busy this morning and last night, but I wouldn't tell her that.

Kiera tilted her head to the side and raised an eyebrow. Her body posture perked up. "Busy, hey?"

My face grew hot as I hugged my feet. "Yeah, busy." Oh, wouldn't you want to know.

She took a seat beside me. "So where is he? Ian?" She stood again, pacing around. "Hey Ian … Ian," she called down the hallway before coming back to the living room. She half chuckled before sitting. "You've been officially dating for over a month and I have yet to meet this guy. Like he's never here when I drive by." She edged closer to me. "So where is he?"

I sighed. "He will be right back. He just ran to the store." I grinned from cheek to cheek. "And he's making me dinner."

Kiera plopped down on the couch, propping her feet on the coffee table. "Well, I'm staying put until he gets here."

I opened my mouth to object. Like my mother, Kiera was a little over the top, and I didn't want to scare him away. I gulped.

Kiera glared at me and rolled her eyes. "Relax, Dany," she said as she rose and headed toward the kitchen. "I'm going to get something to drink."

I didn't respond. She had no problem making herself at home and I had no problem letting her. She was like a sister to me, but I was still a little on guard since she wasn't there for me when she was dating that piece of crap.

She returned to the living room with a soda and cracked it open. "So are you two like serious, serious? In like, he met your mom serious?"

I shrugged. "He met my mother briefly when she showed up early one morning."

Kiera choked on her drink. "Your mom caught Ian spending the night?" She forced back a small laugh. "Damn, right."

I knew what she was thinking. I didn't really want my mom's first time meeting Ian to be him waking up on a Saturday morning when we weren't even a couple. I think she was just glad I was getting out there at all. She hadn't said anything and hadn't bombarded me with twenty questions. Or maybe she was waiting for me to acknowledge we were now a thing. I got goosebumps just thinking about it.

Kiera looked behind me out the window just as I heard a car pull up. "Is his the white car?"

I jumped up. "Yup, that is him." I rubbed my hands together. "I wonder what he bought."

"Never mind the food. I need to meet him in the flesh. I want to know what you see in him."

I cringed. "Flesh" was such an off-putting word. The front door opened and Kiera immediately greeted him.

"Hello, I'm Kiera, the best friend!"

Ian put down the bags, stared at me and shook her outreached hand. "Hey, I'm Ian."

I interjected myself into the conversation. "Well, since you two already kind of introduced yourselves, I'll make it more formal." I realized how stupid I sounded. "Ian, this is my friend Kiera. I have known her forever, and Kiera, well, this is Ian, my boyfriend. The one I talked about constantly."

Ian stood there, blushing a bit. "It's nice to meet you, Kiera."

"You too, Ian," Kiera replied. "Don't worry, I'm not going to stay very long. Promise. Danyelle said you were making her some delicious food. It's so nice to have a man who cooks."

"I try," Ian said sheepishly.

"No really, it's cool. I always wished my ex would cook."

I rolled my eyes. No one wanted to know about her ex. That egoistical piece of crap who alienated her from all her family and friends? Ugh, screw him.

Ian's face grew hot.

I reached over and gave him a hug and whispered. "Why won't you take the bags to the kitchen?"

He responded with a kiss on the forehead. "Okay."

He picked up the bags, and I took a quick glance as he passed. As expected, he had picked up some eggplant along with some brown package. Some kind of meat. I was excited.

When he exited through the living room, Kiera leaned over to me. "He's cute."

I whispered back. "I know."

"Not what I expected from someone who drove without a license."

I shot her a glance and told her to hush as Ian returned back in sight. I trudged on toward him, and we all took a seat.

"So, Ian," Kiera said, as she crossed her legs and leaned back. "Dany told me you are a plumber?" She prodded at her sleeve with a smug look on her face.

Ian nodded. "Yeah."

She twirled her fingers around her hair and pulled. "So, you clean toilets for a living?" She smirked, and I shot her a "stop being an ass" glance.

"Kiera!" I shouted. *What kind of question was that?*

"What? It's a legit question."

She should be grateful I didn't roll my eyes to the back of my head. "It's a stupid question."

Ian stared at her, hiding a smirk. "I install toilets. I'm not a janitor."

Kiera grew red. "Well . . . that's good. Plumbers make good money."

Ian glanced at me and back at Kiera. "So how about I ask you something?"

Kiera glanced at me and smiled. "What, Mr. Janitor?"

Ian leaned his elbows on his knees. "Are you the friend who set up Dany and my first date?"

Kiera opened her mouth to respond, but remained quiet. She glanced away, face beet red.

"I'll take your silence as a yes." Ian leaned back, a strange smile on his face. "It's okay, nothing to be embarrassed about. It was just a question."

Kiera shifted from foot to foot before she turned and stared at him. Her hands were planted on her hips, and her piercing eyes frowned at the corners. "I did you two a favor. Danyelle was never going to ask you out and I highly doubt you were going to. So, I helped you out. If anything, you should be thanking me for bringing you together."

Ian chortled. "Thanks, I guess."

She fiddled with the strap of her tank, grumbled something, and looked at the time. "Well, I better get going." She stood, took a deep breath, and let out an exaggerated sigh. "It was nice meeting you, Mr. Janitor . . . Ian."

"It's nice to meet you too."

Kiera turned to me. "Text you later."

"Sounds good. Talk soon."

Kiera didn't say another word as she left. As soon as the front door closed behind her, I burst into laughter. "Should have seen her face."

"Yeah, she didn't seem pleased. Sorry."

I placed my hand on his shoulder. "Don't be."

He reached over and kissed me. "Any more surprise visitors?"

"I hope not."

He embraced me again. "So how about I make you a delicious lunch?

"Can I help?" I asked quickly.

"No, just kick back and relax." He smiled again.

"Yes, sir."

He kissed me and headed into the kitchen. I took this time to go grab my phone from the other room. If Ian wanted to pamper me and make me a homemade meal, who was I to stop him? I headed into the living room with my cell in hand.

There were twelve missed texts from Kiera. One from five minutes ago.

You told him about me setting you two up.

I sighed. I hadn't told her, but the truth was, I didn't tell him. *He figured it out,* I texted back. *He asked me point blank if I was the one who sent the message. I couldn't lie.*

Ian was very good at reading people. There was no explanation on how he would have known or even put two and two together that I wasn't the one to send that message. To a normal person, it wouldn't have crossed their mind. But it did him. I always wondered if that meant all along he could sense I liked him and was nervous.

He is kind of rude.

I rolled my eyes at that. Had she forgotten how much of an ass her ex was? How he complained and made fun of all her friends, and not to mention, treated her like crap. Ian wasn't mean like that. He was shy and said nothing the majority of the time. But it was Kiera who'd asked a stupid question.

He answered your question, didn't he?

A few seconds later my phone pinged.

Pft. Yeah, but he was kind of cheeky about it. But I do give it to you, he is a gentleman. I just hope his cooking is as good as he is on the eyes. Because damn, he's cute.

Oh, you have no idea.

Out of nowhere, Ian walked back into the kitchen.

"What's up?" I asked.

"I have a few extra minutes to come see you."

"Oh?" I said.

"Did I catch you in the middle of a top secret conversation?" Ian laughed at his own joke. Man, Ian didn't realize how much fun he was when he just loosened up. He almost seemed like an entirely different person.

"It was just Kiera," I laughed. "She says you are cute."

He raised an eyebrow. "Cute? I guess that wasn't the word I'd choose for myself."

"You *are* good looking. It all means the same thing."

He glanced back toward the kitchen. "I'll leave you to your conversation. I should get back."

"Yes. I'm excited for what you are making." I could smell garlic all the way from over here. "Whatever it is, it smells yummy."

He was already in the kitchen before I was able to finish my sentence. I half wanted to get up and go sneak and find out what he was making. But I wouldn't. If he wanted me to know, then I'd know.

He is damn fine. Not only is he sexy, he is smart and kind. He really is so sweet.

I wasn't one to be shallow, but it was icing on the cake. Ian had well defined abs, a nice smile, and he wasn't an asshole. That was a bonus.

Does your mom know about how you two met? Wink.

The pit in my stomach tightened. She didn't know, and I had no intentions of telling her the truth.

I told her we met at the auto body shop.

I know you mentioned she met him briefly, right? What has she said about him?

I circled my finger around the screen. She hadn't really said much.

She says he is a nice young man. Besides that, not much.

I stood and paced. Eventually I would need to make a formal introduction between Mom and Ian. I just remember the day my sister brought home her boyfriend. She quizzed him about everything from where he worked to what school he went to and what grades he got. She even had the audacity to ask if his parents worked. My sister was mortified, and their relationship didn't last. She claimed it was because they weren't meant to be, but I knew better. Mom scared him off.

I just hoped she wouldn't ruin things for me. Ian wasn't open about talking about his family, and I'm not sure how he'd handle my *mother* and how she was. If she asked him where he was from, would he easily give it up to her? He hid his feelings really well from me. I took a deep breath. I was overthinking it. I'd just warn him and see what he wanted to do.

"Are you all right?"

I jumped and turned to look at Ian. "Yeah, I was just thinking."

"Well, lunch is ready, if you want to come eat."

All my floundering went on the back burner as I followed him into my kitchen.

"I made stuffed eggplant with minced pork, some spices, cheese, and a hint of hot sauce," he said. Then he turned to a second plate. "And a garden salad with my homemade vinaigrette."

It wasn't my typical meal, but it looked delicious, and it was something I hadn't tried before. Well, except a salad, but I was excited to try it.

Ian took the two trays and a couple of forks into the living room. We sat at the coffee table. "Try some."

I took the fork from him and scooped a mouthful of the filling from the eggplant. It was very good. I took another bite.

"This is very good. Where did you learn to cook?"

"Self-taught."

"It's pretty amazing."

"Thanks," he said as his face blushed. "I just wanted to impress you."

"Well you did, because you are so talented. You don't give yourself enough credit."

So my original assumptions were correct, Ian was just as insecure as I was. We were so much alike. I appreciated having someone who understood me, even if he didn't know it.

9

Ian showed up a few minutes before noon dashing, and handsome as ever wearing a button up charcoal dress shirt tucked into a pair of navy pants. Last night Mom had invited Ian and I over for dinner. I knew it was coming and I told him so. Ian said it would be fine, but I couldn't tell how he felt through text.

I cleared my throat. "Ready?" I pressed my lips together, shuffling from foot to foot. My mom was overbearing and he would be subjected to an interrogated while she made her opinion of him. "Just remember how we *met.*"

Ian nodded. "We met at an auto body shop. It'll be fine, Danyelle. Take a deep breath." He put his hands on my shoulders and kissed me on the forehead. "It won't be that bad."

"You are right." Only he didn't know my mother like I did. But I'm happy he dressed up for me. Mom was peculiar like I was, only in a more supercilious way.

"So..." Ian pressed. "Are we going?"

I cleared my throat again. "Yeah. Let me grab my keys."

Ian didn't say anything, and his expression didn't really tell me anything either. He seemed cool and collected. I wondered how he'd react, or what he'd say when Mom asked him about his parents or his childhood. I told him how overbearing she was and how she'd be similar to a job interview. I was almost relieved I didn't have to meet his parents, as selfish as that sounded.

Inside my car I turned on the air conditioning. Ian stared at the touch screen on the dash.

"Your car is nice."

In the three and half months we have been dating, he has never set foot in my car. I just mentioned we take my vehicle to reduce the number of awkward questions from the upcoming dinner. "I like the built in GPS," I replied. Ian's car was an older model Honda but as he told me it works and he could get around easily. He didn't have any debt and that was a good thing in the grand scheme of things.

"If it isn't too late would you want to catch a late night movie?" Ian asked as I drove.

"Yeah, sure."

"Take a deep breath. I'm sure your mom isn't that bad."

I glanced over to him and smiled. "You're right."

We arrived at my parents' house. They lived in a quiet area of the city, near the edge in more of an older generation neighborhood. Mom insisted on moving when we all moved out. She wanted simpler living as she said, but what she really meant she wanted quality over quantity.

Ian wiped some sweat off his forehead. So he was a bit more nervous than he lead on.

"So let's go."

We walked up the path, lined with little shrubs and flowers to the front door. I knocked on the door, smoothed over my blouse before opening the door.

Dad greeted us at the doorway. "Oh, hello, Danyelle." He hugged me. I had no idea he was even going to be home. He often was out fishing or out on the road with the guys since he retired from the stock market a few years back. A load lifted off my shoulders, though. Mom seemed more mellow when Dad was around.

"It's good to see you Dad." I gently pulled Ian inside. "Dad, this is Ian. Ian this is my dad."

Ian held out his hand and they shook. "It's nice to meet you Ian."

"You as well Mr. Fitzgerald."

"Call me Robert."

Ian nodded sheepishly.

I took off my shoes and followed Dad up the steps to the living room. Ian followed closely behind. I took a seat on the loveseat. Up until a few years ago Mom was particular about us sitting on her furniture. She called it her 'look' couch. She had decorative pillows and a cover and told us it was for shows. I never understood that. Who the hell wanted a piece of furniture they couldn't sit on or use?

Mom came out of the kitchen with a pot of tea. "It's so nice to see you again, Ian."

"You as well, Mrs. Fitzgerald."

She frowned. "Now, now. Call me Sharla."

"Sorry, yes Sharla. It's very nice to see you again." Ian face flushed. He was so polite and composed. It was a totally one eighty of his more laid back personality.

She poured Ian a cup of tea, and handed to him. "It's no nice to formally meet. I know you and Dany have busy schedules but it's so nice to sit down and get to know the wonderful young man she has brought into her life."

Ian trembled a bit, but otherwise kept his front. "I'm glad to have met her too."

Dad sat beside Mom and smiled. "So what do you do for a living, Ian?"

Ian straightened his shoulders. "I work as a commercial plumber over at A & D plumbing."

Dad rubbed the back of his neck. "I don't recall that company. Where about is it located?" I bit my lip, my nerves spiking again. Dad was easier going then Mom, but still he had his standards.

Ian came steady eye contact with Dad. "It's a relatively new shop downtown. I've been working there for a few years after they opened up shop."

Dad smirked. "I'll be sure to check it out next time we need some services done."

"Oh you get the 10% family discount, but you know, you can always call me off the clock and I'll do whatever, you know, for Dany's parents…haha!"" Ian said. I stomped on his foot to get him to shup up. I hopedg they didn't take it the wrong way.

Mom smiled. "Now aren't you a generous young man."

Ian posture softened. "Thank you."

"Well, dinner will be ready soon. I hoped you're all hungry." Mom rose and headed to the kitchen.

"We should move into the dining room," Dad said, and without a word we followed him into the other room. I was delighted Mom made a light but sophisticated dinner. She prepared smoked tuna, and some steamed asparagus along with some caviar. Sheesh, did she realize she was having lunch to officially meet my boyfriend not fine dining? Dots of sweat beaded my forehead. I wondered if she was trying to intimate him.

She dished herself some fish before passing it to Ian on her right. "So, Ian, Danyelle tells me you two met at an auto body shop. Were you involved in an accident as well?"

Ian shook his head. "No, I was just having some repairs done on my car."

I took some caviar before passing it on.

Mom turned to me and winked. "I guess your fender bender was destined to happen."

I half-heartedly laughed. "Yeah." The pit in my stomach tightened. I hated lying about how we actually met. "I'd say it was destined."

Ian patted my thigh.

I forced a mouthful of fish in my mouth.

"So how long have you lived in the city?" Mom asked him.

Ian flinched. "Several years. I moved here from a small town in Alaska."

Mom raised her eyebrow. "Alaska? What would bring you to these parts? A change of weather I'd say."

"Mom?" I mumbled.

"Now, now Danyelle. I'm sure Alaska is fine." She turned her focus back to Ian. "So your family is from Alaska? How do your parents feel about you being all the way of here?"

I could feel his leg bouncing. "My parents passed away when I was young. I really didn't have any other family. There wasn't much in terms of employment so I moved across country for a new start. New weather, new opportunities, and I didn't need to drive through Canada to get to other states…"

Ian didn't tell me that he couldn't' find work in Alaska. I mean it made sense with how isolated the state was. And I had looked up it had one of the highest crimes rates in the country. So his reasons were plausible, but why hadn't he told me?

Mom frowned. "I'm sorry to hear. I couldn't imagine. I'm sure they were good people."

I sat there with my mouth wide open. I was tired of her prying.

Ian glanced downward. "They were fine." He sounded sad. He took a sip of the tea Mom had given him.

"So how do you like it here?" Mom asked.

Why couldn't she just give him a break? He just told her his parents were dead. Why couldn't she just drop it, stop interrogating him and let him have a moment to breathe.

"The weather is nice. Lots of jobs and well then there is Danyelle. Another awesome reason to be here."

A warm feeling emerged on the inside. Ian knew just what to say. Dad smiled so Ian was making a good impression. When my sister had brought home a boyfriend Dad didn't approve of one time, he frowned and made excuses to go to the bathroom. But the real question was, how did Mom feel? Did he make a good impression for her?

Mom took a sip of tea. "I see. So you bought a house, I take it?"

I nearly choked. "Mom, can you pass me some more tea?" I interrupted, but Ian deserved a break from twenty questions.

"Oh, for sure dear." She raised an eyebrow as she passed the tea kettle over to me. I filled up my cup and sat the kettle back on a coaster.

"So Mom, is Saoirse around?" Usually my cousin was around when I ame over.

Mom shook her head. "No, she went to spend the day with your Aunt Carol, you know, Dad's sister. She is going home in a few days."

"Oh? Is she feeling better?" She was sick for so long and it was only recently the doctor's were able to pin point what it was that was wrong.

Mom straightened on the chair. "Yes. Saoirse is so excited to go home."

"I bet."

Dad checked out the time. "It's almost time for the hockey game. Ian, do you watch sports on television?"

"Sometimes," Ian replied.

"Feel free to stop by at any time to catch the game if you'd like."

I wanted to stand up and shout out in glee. Dad liked him. Dad liked him. I turned to glance at Mom to get a read on her. Did she like Ian? Ian wasn't your typical university grad who owned his own house and had parents who were well off. I didn't even have any idea what his parents did, when they were alive, that was.

"I almost forgot," Mom said. "You were telling me about your living arrangements."

I swore under my breath. I hoped she had forgotten about that. It wasn't any of her business.

"I'm renting right now. I'm saving for a generous down payment on a house," Ian said. "I just wanted to establish a good paying job before I was thirty, and since I accomplished that with a few months to spare, saving for a house is my next step."

I tapped my foot on the floor, and forced myself to not show how annoyed I was. Ian told me he didn't want a mortgage. He got mad at me when I asked him about it, but here he was telling my parents he was saving for a down payment. I rubbed my brow as if I was trying to ward off an oncoming headache. All I knew was Ian and I needed to have a talk. I needed him to be vulnerable with me. I couldn't live with the secrets following him around. I couldn't do it. I just needed to know what he wanted for the future, what his plans were for us, for our future. We were getting serious and I could picture us ten, twenty, even thirty plus years from now, but on the other hand there was still a huge question mark following him around. I knew what he liked, what he didn't like, his hobbies, but his childhood and where he came from. Was he just afraid to open up with me? Was it something I did, or said?

"Danyelle, are you allright?" Mom asked me.

I escaped my floundering to Ian, and turned to see my dad and mom staring at me. "Yeah, sorry…" I mumbled.

"Well, I'm just going to clean up. It was so nice for you to come by. It was a pleasure to get to know Ian better," my mom said as she started gathering the plates.

"Here let me help," Ian said as he reached for the remaining dishes.

"No, no. You are our guest. But it's so nice for you to offer, Ian."

I looked at the grandfather clock in the wall in the dining area. It was hitting two in the afternoon and I was inching to leave and do something, anything outside of these four walls. I wanted to confront, or I mean discuss, with Ian how I felt.

"We should probably be getting going. I have an order for a client I need to work on." I lied yet again. It was convenient, but how else could I leave without making Mom feel like I was avoiding her?

"Oh, I won't keep you two." Mom gave me a hug and then Ian who accepted it. He seemed to be comfortable and a little more open then I had bargained.

"It was nice seeing you again, Sharla."

On the way out, Ian stopped to say farewell to my dad. Dad shook his hand firmly before we left.

Once the fresh air hit us on the way out, instantly I felt relieved. In the driver's seat I took a huge deep breath.

"It wasn't that bad. It wasn't that bad," I whispered to myself.

"Are you all right?" Ian asked concerned.

I clenched my jaw. "Why did you tell my mother you were saving for a mortgage? When you told me you didn't want to have any debt?"

It came out abruptly and I almost regretted it because of my tone alone.

Ian shuffled in his seat. "I said it for you."

I started the car and pulled away not responding. What did he mean he did it for me?

"You were worried about what your mother would think. So I played it up. I said what I thought she'd wanted to hear." He sighed. "But I really don't think it was necessary."

I shot back. "So why did you say it then?"

He shrugged. "You lied to her about how we met, so I decided to just keep up with that image you wanted to portray. But I think you over think it. Your parents are very nice. They acted how I pictured a concerned parent would when meeting their daughter's boyfriend for the first time."

Little did he know just how my mother could be? She was tame. One time she asked my sister's one boyfriend when we were fifteen and seventeen respectively if his parents were criminals. Before my grandfather retired as police chief, Mom had him do background checks on all our friends' parents.

"I guess. She is usually a lot more overbearing."

Ian let out an exasperated breath. "It almost feels like you are embarrassed by me."

I pulled over to the side of the road and put the car in park. "Is that what you really think?" I watched him furtively, crossing my arms. "Do you really think I'm embarrassed by you? Seriously? If I was embarrassed by you, I wouldn't be with you." I turned away and took several deep labor breaths and pulled at my sleeves. He didn't understand. It wasn't him; it was my parents. They wouldn't understand.

"Then why do you worry so much about what they think?"

"Because." I poked my tongue lightly into my cheek an inhaled a long breath. "They are judgmental. If my mom knew how we really met she'd instantly not like you. She would automatically assume the worst. When she saw my car, she called me, and I brushed it off. She was talking like I had lost a leg. Heck, growing up I wasn't allowed to hang out with anyone who didn't come from their circle. " I inhaled sharply. It was a touchy subject. I loved my mom and wanted her approval. I wanted her to love Ian as much as I did.

Ian caressed my hand. "Maybe they trust your judgement. I'm sorry for accusing you of being embarrassed by me. I guess I just don't understand."

"I just wished I understood more about you," I blurted out. "And did your parents really die?"

"There is nothing left to say about them. They aren't in my life. I don't want to talk about them. Let's talk about something else." He crossed his arms. "Or let's just go back to your house. I 'm tired and think I'll go home and have a nap."

I turned back on the car and pulled away. There he went again and shut down. Maybe he just needed a little more time.

We drove in silence. Every few moments I looked over at Ian looking out the window. When we pulled up in front of my house, I said. "I appreciated you going to my parent's house for lunch. It meant a lot."

Ian looked over to me. "I'd do anything for you."
I reached over and kissed him. He'd do anything but the one thing I really wanted from him. I wanted him to tell me where he came from. Who was he?

10

It had been four and half months, and I still didn't know anything about Ian beyond that he came from Alaska and met Waylon here in this city. And that his birthday was next month. He was turning thirty.

It didn't help that my mother had met him, and he somehow was able to answer her invasive questions with ease without even flinching. But I knew better. I appreciated that Ian was patient and wasn't scared off. He didn't complain, and he told me my mother was nice. Little did he know, she was studying him, internally making notes of what she liked and didn't like about him.

I was trying my best to be patient, but I wasn't sure if I could do this anymore. I knew Ian was a handyman and a great kisser. We got along so well, but he still had so many question marks following him around. He had very few friends and spent most of his time at home. Why? What was he hiding? Maybe I was just overthinking it. Maybe he was just a loner or shy. Maybe he just didn't like crowds. Would he have gone out with someone like me if it wasn't because of circumstance?

Ian came into the kitchen behind me. "What's wrong?"

I didn't say anything as he wrapped his arms around me. I flinched.

"You've been on edge all morning. Would you like me to leave?"

I shook my head. "I just wish I knew more about you."

Ian bit his upper lip. "What do you want to know? I mean, I told you everything that's important." He evaded my eye contact. "I don't want to bore you."

I stood akimbo and frowned. "Whenever I ask you about your life back in Alaska, you get upset or change the subject. Why?"

Ian planted a soft kiss on my forehead. "I'm not hiding anything." His voice was soft, but he avoided my gaze. "I just don't like talking about my family."

I sighed and backed up slightly. I didn't know if I could keep this up without knowing anything about him. He knew everything about *my* family. He met my mother, after all, and that was a big deal, but he wouldn't — or, as he said many times, couldn't — tell me one single thing about his family. "I just want to know you. Where you came from. How do you expect us to be together if you won't tell me anything about you? It just feels like a one-way street."

Ian ran his hand through his hair and mumbled. "Fine."

He trembled as he stared at the fridge behind me.

I stood, waiting for his answer. He didn't make eye contact and took a deep breath.

"My mother died of a drug overdose, and my father was so depressed that he drank himself to death a few years later. I practically took care of myself. There is really nothing else to say. I have no family and only bad memories of that place." His hands curled into fists and then straightened as he mumbled something I couldn't quite make out.

My insides twisted. "You had no friends out there. Anyone?" I pushed further. I couldn't put my finger on it, but it felt like he was holding something else back. The anguish crossing his face didn't match the indifference he managed to muster. He was struggling, I could tell.

"I have no friends out there. None that matter, anyway . .
." His voice trailed off, almost inaudible. He shifted from foot
to foot as he fiddled with his collar. "You don't understand,
Danyelle."

My jaw clenched and my posture tightened. "What don't I
understand?" I just wanted him to tell me the truth.

"You don't understand what it's like to have parents who
don't give two shits about you. It's better not to talk about
them. So please, can you just drop it? Please. I don't want to
talk about it anymore."

I glanced downward. "Okay, I'm sorry. I'll leave it alone."

I reached over and embraced him. I wouldn't bring it up
again, but in the back of my mind, there was something still
bothering me.

One thing was for sure: he was hiding something.
Someone or something from Alaska haunted him, and I
needed to know what—or who—it was. I didn't want to
snoop or appear overbearing, but there was something
nagging me, and I just wanted to know what it was, even if it
was just to understand him better.

I released him from my grasp. "I'm sorry for bringing it
up. I didn't mean…"

"It's fine." He pulled away slightly. "Do you mind if I
have a shower? I just need some time alone."

"For sure."

Ian disappeared up the stairs. I hated that he was upset
with me, but at least he still felt at home. He could have
easily just left and went home to shower.

After a minute with my head in the clouds, I headed
upstairs to my bedroom to relax. I retrieved my laptop from
on top of my end table by the bed. The shower was on, and I
really wanted to join him, but stopped short. He'd said he
wanted to be alone.

I hovered over my screen, carefully listening to make sure
the shower wasn't off. In the search engine I typed in his
name, Ian Fogg, and the place he came from, Alaska.

I scrolled through the search results. I came across obituaries. I scrolled through the archives when I came across Mary Fogg, who passed away on July 9, 2003, at the age of thirty-nine. I did the quick math in my head. That was 16 years ago. So, if Ian was turning thirty next month, he'd be fourteen when she passed. My stomach churned. I couldn't imagine losing my mother so young. I scanned the rest of the obituary. It didn't mention anything about Ian or about his father.

I next tried to search for anyone else who had passed away with the last name Fogg. I came up empty. I did take note of the town Mary Fogg passed away in. I returned and narrowed my search to Ian Fogg and that particular town in Alaska.

I scrolled through some more, until I heard the shower turn off. I swore a little as I scrolled faster. I didn't want him to catch me searching, but I was so close. I could feel the truth on the tip of my fingers. I stared back at the screen, scrolling until I finally stopped at the headline: *Graduating year of 2007.*

I clicked on the page. Ian was still in the bathroom and was making no sudden movements. I still had time. I looked at the yearbook and scrolled until I stopped at Ian Fogg. There was no picture attached. Maybe he'd missed school that day.

I kept scrolling, and a picture caught my eye. It was Ian. He was younger, but it was definitely him. I recognized his eyes and expression. He was lanky, but it was him. He was standing beside another young man. He was several inches shorter. He looked so sad. His shoulders were drooped, and it appeared he lacked any energy.

I stared at the picture. Ian said he didn't have any friends, but clearly this person was a friend. Why else would they be in the same photo together? They obviously went to the same high school, as they were both dressed in regalia.

I heard a sigh and his heavy breathing. I jumped and turned to make eye contact with Ian. He stood behind me with just a towel wrapped around his waist. He was staring at the screen. I didn't know what to say.

Ian's shoulders slumped. He looked like he had seen a ghost.

"I—I . . ."

"Where did you find that?" Ian asked abruptly. A little too curt for my liking.

I bowed my head. "I'm sorry, Ian. I just wanted to learn more about you. It was difficult for you to talk about it, so I just wanted to do a little digging. "

He bit his lip. "So, what did you find out?"

Sweat drenched Ian from head to toe. He wasn't angry, but he was anxious. What was he worried about? Did he do something stupid like shoplift or did the guy he was with do something stupid, and he was too embarrassed to talk about it? Or maybe I was overthinking it.

"Is Mary your mother?"

Ian looked away. "Yeah." He paced the room back and forth a bit. "She died, like I told you, from a drug overdose. I'm still surprised anyone cared enough to make an obituary for her."

"I'm sorry," I said.

Ian's fists clenched and unclenched. "I just don't like talking about it. About her."

I nodded and apologized again. But there was still the question about the guy he was with. "Is this your friend? Brother?"

Ian sat down beside me. "Let me see."

I handed him the laptop and he stared at the screen. His bottom lip trembled. "That's Brody Crane." He looked away for a second. "He was my best friend and the reason I left that place."

I sat there, wanting to press further. Where was Brody now? What happened? And why was it the reason why he left his home, where he grew up? It had nothing to do with the cold, that much I assumed.

"I don't want to talk about it, Dany. But you are stubborn," he smiled slightly, and then frowned. "So, I'd rather you hear it from me than some news article and biased bullshit."

I rubbed his thigh and said nothing.

"It was Brody's twenty-first birthday and he wanted to get smashed. We were drunk. He wanted more booze, and I was too out of it to stop him. So he left, and I passed out." Ian stopped to catch a breath. "Around four in the morning, I was a little more sober. I know what you are thinking, but I was stupid back then. But I went out looking for him. Didn't find him. So, I went back to his place and passed back out. Figured he'd show up in the morning."

Ian's lips pressed tightly in a grimace, and his shoulders dropped as he hunched over. He shook his head.

"He didn't come back, did he?" I whispered. I reached over and wrapped my arm around him.

"No, he didn't." Ian rocked back and forth. "I found out later that day that his car went over a cliff. They never found his body. His parents, like mine, didn't give two shits." His whole posture tightened, and he balled his hands into fists. "There were search parties, and they didn't attend one. After a week, they presumed he drowned. So, they just wrote him off as dead. I—I just don't get it." He got up off the bed and paced.

I reached over and closed out of the internet screen. "I'm sorry. You don't need to tell me anymore. I shouldn't have pressed so far."

Ian stopped pacing, and he was drenched in sweat. "That is why I left Alaska. I couldn't live with the guilt. I couldn't deal with knowing I didn't stop him. I did a few odd jobs, saved up some money, bought a plane ticket, and flew to Seattle. I used what little money I had left and hopped on a bus to get here. I met Waylon and he helped me out. He rented me a room and got me a job with a friend of his. And that is my life story." He shrugged. "Shitty childhood, best friend died, so I didn't have a choice. I left."

I couldn't wrap my mind around it all. The pit in my stomach tightened. No wonder he didn't want to talk about it. I wouldn't want to talk about it either if my best friend drove over a cliff and their body was never found. And to think Brody's parents didn't care enough to keep looking for their son. And Ian. Tears threatened to emerge. He had nobody. He left town and no one noticed. No one cared.

One thing I knew for sure was that Ian was right. I didn't know what it was like to have parents who didn't care. My mom and dad were overbearing and had high expectations for me, but they were always there.

When I was a kid, if I scraped my knee, my mom was right there to make me feel better. She spent countless hours helping me with homework, was there for every reward, and cheered me on at every graduation.

I just couldn't imagine how Ian felt. I was sheltered and had never met or associated with someone who came from that side of the tracks. I hadn't known anyone whose parents were addicts. I wasn't even allowed to have friends whose parents were unemployed.

Ian lay face down on the bed, texting someone. I wanted to ask him who, but I didn't say anything. My guess was it was Waylon. When he was stressed or needed help, Waylon was there. How do I compete with that?

The worst part about it was I was still holding something inside. I didn't trust him or myself enough to tell him about New Year's Eve.

"How do you feel?" Ian asked out of the blue.

It caught me off guard. "About?"

"Me?" he said. "Does it change how you feel about me? Knowing what you know now?"

I shook my head. "Of course not." I fiddled with the collar of my shirt. "Alcohol is evil. And I'm sorry you blame yourself for Brody's death, but it wasn't your fault."

Does it mean it wasn't my fault that I woke up without any recollection beside a man I barely knew after a night of drinking?

"How do you figure it wasn't my fault?" Ian pressed, his face contorted.

I took a deep breath. "It is no one's fault. You were both drinking, and people do stupid things while drinking. You couldn't have known that would have happened. I know how it feels to drink and mess up. So, don't blame yourself. I know that's hard, but don't."

Ian nodded. "I can't help it."

"I should know," I whispered. I began to tremble but forced myself to keep it together.

Ian glanced at me, placing a hand on my arm. "What do you mean?"

I took a deep breath. He told me something personal and the least I could do was do the same. "On New Year's Eve, I had a lot to drink, and I woke up the next morning beside a man I barely knew. I had no idea how I got there, or really anything about that night. I don't remember consenting or anything. I blamed myself for putting myself in that situation, but now I realize I couldn't have predicted that would happen." I stopped and took a deep breath. "I'm not sure why I'm telling you this, Ian."

Ian pulled me into his arms. "I'm sorry that happened." He held me tight before pulling me back so that we made eye contact. "Any man who would have sex with a woman who is unable to consent is a shitty person."

I felt my resolve crumble as tears streamed down my cheeks. Why, I didn't know. It felt so surreal.

Ian pulled away, held his hands on the side of my shoulders, and stared deep into my eyes. "I love you."

I stood there, my mouth agape. "What?"

"I love you," Ian repeated. "Just for being there for me. For understanding me and not judging me."

So many emotions were going through my head. So much was happening. I cared about him so much. I just never expected those three words from him—from Ian, the most complicated, closed-off man I had ever met. But he said it. I always thought it would have been me.

My stomach filled with butterflies. "I love you, too."

Ian reached in and we kissed. It was only right.

11

Ian and I had seen each other every day this week. If he wasn't at work, he was at my house. Over the course of the last few months, his posessions found there way in each crook and cranny. I created a spot in my sewing room for his clothing, and his own 'junk drawer' in my kitchen. He even brought his own pillow to stay at my house. I crawled my way carefully from under Ian's arm, planting my feet on the floor. Ian flinched but rolled over. On the way out in the hallway, I tripped over one of his shoes. Thankfully I caught myself from planting face first into the ground.

I headed down to the kitchen to start a pot of coffee. Ian would likely wake up, notice I was gone and come downstairs. I soon learned he liked to sleep in, where I naturally woke up early but since meeting him I had started to naturally change my schedule as had he to accommodate one another.

As predicted, ten minutes later, wearing just boxers, Ian walked in the kitchen. He sported crazy bed hair and a smirk. "Why did I have a feeling you'd be in here?"

I snickered. "Making you're lazybehind some coffee."

The timer dinged just in time as he plopped on the chair. I poured us each a cup and I sat across from him. "Did you sleep well?"

Ian nodded. "Yeah." He yawned. "I usually don't wake up before noon on my days off."

I rolled my eyes. "Well half the day is gone by then." It was the same conversation every Saturday morning after our first few weekends together. I took a sip from the mug. "What do you want to do today?"

Ian shrugged. "Maybe go back to bed?"

I frowned. "Seriously? How about we take a walk somewhere. Or maybe check out the street fair downtown or maybe we could do something cool like rock climbing?"

Ian flinched, his face turned red and looked away.

I gave him a puzzled look. "What's wrong? Are you scared of heights?" I joked.

Ian shook his head. "Just the last time I went rock climbing, I was super drunk. And let's just say I swore to never rock climb again."

"Oh, this is a story I need to hear." The more I stared into his eyes, the more he blushed. When he didn't answered, I added, "Now, come on spit it out."

"Well…" he twisted his mug in his hands. "I fell face first into a bush, and sliced my arm open,l and it required a few stitches. I thought once I got to the top I'd be like superman. It was for a co-worker's birthday party I got suckered into attending." He showed me his upper arm where he showed me a fading scar.

"So you were acting like an idiot."

Ian bowed his head. "I guess, so yeah. What's wrong with being super man? Maybe you could be super woman, and we could pretend to fly."

"You mean you want us to act like drunken fools?"

Ian got up to fix himself another cup. "A walk sounds nice."

Once he sat down again, I moved over next to him and shuffled the seat over. He smiled. I touched the side of his face. His cheeks were warm and his eye contact strong. I kissed him softly.

A silly grin crossed his face cheek to cheek. "Unless you have something else in mind?"

"No — just a walk is fine."

So maybe I was teasing him. He shot a yearning look my way. I knew he likely wanted to go back to bed, but I really wanted to go out and do things. I liked spending quality time with him both in public and in bed. We needed a balance.

"Why don't we go get dressed and go out? How does that sound?"

Ian nodded. "Okay." He reached over and kissed me on the forehead.

We finished our coffee and headed for the bedroom. The temptation to rip off his boxers and jump in bed excited me. Filled me with yearning. Ian was very good in bed. He made me feel so warm, so secure. I never imagined in a million years that the man who didn't have a driver's license, who had driving illegally when we met, would end up my boyfriend. We were so great together. Kiera's jealousy, in a bittersweet, but almost satisfying way, was icing on the cake.

I rummaged through my closet for something to wear. It was supposed to be a hundred degrees outside, so a hot day. I picked up a summer dress. I slipped my pajama top up and over my head and replaced it with the floral, knee length dress.

I turned around to catch Ian staring. He blushed and quickly put his shirt on.

"What you looking at?" I teased.

"Nothing. Just getting dressed," he looked around sarcastically, "you know, enjoying the décor in the room…"

I stood with my hands on my hips. "Décor?" I laughed. "Bullshit."

He couldn't contain a smile as he made a quick glance around the room once more. "I was just admiring your orange blinds. Getting into the Halloween spirit. You know?"

I half frowned and pursed my lips, but I was amused anyway. "You can be my theme." I got up and headed for the door. "I'm going to brush my hair. So hurry and get dressed."

After throwing my hair back into a ponytail, I put on some blush and lip gloss, I rubbed the back of my nape. If we were going to go for a walk, maybe I could pack a picnic lunch for us to enjoy on our walk. I wanted to disconnect myself from the outside world and enjoy a day with my hunny. Ian entered the bathroom behind me and wrapped his hands around me. "What are you thinking about?"

"Food."

I studied his expression in the mirror.

"Food?"

"I'm going to pack us a picnic lunch. I think going for a hike or a long walk would do us both good. And we all know you eat like a pig."

"I got to eat."

I rolled my eyes. "Of course. So what do you want to eat, besides sandwiches, which is what I'm going to pack?"

"Eggplant?" He smirked. "Eggplant soup... Eggplant deep-fried."

I sighed. "Seriously."

"Water bottles, maybe some fruit, raisins maybe...." Ian gaze adverted.

"I got some trail mix," I suggested. I stared at Ian as he nodded. There was that look again. He was about to say something but drifted off and shut down. What was he keeping inside? What was he afraid to talk about?

I reached over and brushed my fingers down his arm.

He flinched and jumped. "A picnic is good. Here let me help you pack." His words jumbled together. He startled.

I frowned slightly. "Okay." There he went again. One of his mood swings. There was something going through his mind and I suspected he wouldn't share what it was with me.

Inside the kitchen, he made a racket as he started to open and close all the cupboards, one right after the other. He had no problem making himself at home, which made me feel warm and fuzzy inside. What would it be like to have him here every day?

"Third cupboard on the left," I suggested.

I focused on making a couple ham and cheese sandwiches, while Ian's trembling hand filled little sandwich bags with trail mix.

"Are you okay?" I finally asked.

Ian nodded and forced a smile. "Yeah, why?"

I wasn't convinced but said, "Just wondering."

Ian bit his upper lip and looked away.

I took the bags from his trembling hands and put them in a lunch kit that hooked to a backpack. "Anything else you think we need?"

"Nope."

"Do you want to drive, or do you want me to?" I asked.

"You can," he admitted. "I'm one payment away from getting my license back, so I really don't want to blow it."

I agreed with him. I could tell something was on his mind but I didn't want to pry. But I did. I would be lying to myself if I tried to convince myself. I just hoped he would tell me what it was. Randomly we'd be having a good moment, and then his mood would change suddenly. He tried to hide it but I knew.

"Let's go."

On the drive to the shore, Ian was more talkative than usual. He was deflecting. I forced a smile but on the inside I wanted to know what was wrong. Nothing happened that would explain his yo-yo of emotions.

When we reached the walking path, I parked. I pulled the packed knapsack from the backseat and we got out.

"Here let's put some sunscreen on. It's supposed to be hot." I retrieved the lotion and lathered a layer on Ian's neck, and arms, and he returned the favor.

"Ready."

Ian held my hand as we walked. There was a slight breeze but mostly it was hot, muggy. I should have brought a hug I thought. Ian didn't seem to mind though. He was wearing a pair of knee length cargo shorts, and a form fitting black tee. It really showed all the contours of his abs. He was yummy.

"Drooling?" Ian let out a little laugh.

My face grew hot, and then I let out a silent sigh, not in his view. One moment he was distant, and the next he is flirty. What was wrong with him today? What was going through his head?

We walked a few miles when we came to two paths. One went up and over a manmade hill and one went directly alongside a small rocky, beach if you want to call it that, along the river. Ian naturally pulled me toward the ocean's edge. I guess that was where we were going. We were lucky we hadn't' gotten much rain this season, considering we lived in a city known for their rain and horrible rainstorms. Flooding was a reality.

Ian gently pulled me ahead, like he was on a mission. I just followed along, waiting, anticipating what he had in mind. We walked several steps when he stopped randomly at little sandy area. There were a few people lounging and soaking up the sun, but otherwise it wasn't too busy.

"Come."

I stood firmly. "Where?"

"In the ocean. It's way too god damn hot, and I don't want to mummify."

I gave him a cheeky smile. I chased after him. I set my backpack several feet from the water, far enough away it didn't get wet, and close enough I could keep my eyes on it.

At the water edge, Ian splashed me. I squealed. A couple in their late twenties turned and stared. I smiled awkwardly, before I splashed Ian back. If a splash war was what he wanted. I'd give it to him.

He pushed water back and for the next minute or two we splashed one another like we were young children having a water war.

All of sudden, Ian picked me up and lifted me out of the water. He had a sinister, devilish smile on his face. He didn't say anything but just the way he pulled me up, I knew what was going to come next.

"Don't you dare!" I yelled, try to remain serious, but I couldn't hold my composure. I blurted laughing. "Ian, I'm warning you." I couldn't stop giggling at him.

"Or what?" he said flirtiously.

"Put me down you scoundrel!" I was nearly choking on my laugher now.

The couple from a few minutes ago stared at us and smiled.

A moment later, he lightly put me down, but I lost my balance and fell backward into the water. My face turned hot as he picked me up out of the water.

"Are you mad?"

I frowned, and then smiled. "No... But just you watch. I'll get you back or so help me…"

Ian smirked, as if he was challenging me, but then all of sudden he sat his ass down in the water. "There. Now we are both wet."

I splashed him once more. "There. We are good!"

He laughed.

He stood, and lifted me off my feet in a big hug as we trekked out of the ocean lines back to the beach. "How about we have something to eat? I'm starving."

We sat on the beach, soaked, sand covering our legs, and probably our food if we even dared set it down. I handed him a sandwich. He wrapped his arm around me pulling me closer, as we ate in silence for a few moments, watching the waves crash against the beach.

No sooner had he devoured his sandwich was he reaching for something else. "This was a good idea," he said.

I nustled my head into his shoulder. For a man with so much mystery, he was so much fun to be with. There was nothing boring about him. My family liked him. My best friend liked him – for the most part. The only last thing I needed to do was get him to open up to me. Let me in. He was the whole package otherwise. Seven months in, and I was smitten.

"I love you," I said.

"I love you, too."

We reached in and kissed tenderly, right there, in the open sun with the waves crashing into the sandy beach and a humming bird singing in the distance.

12

I lay my head on Ian's chest, feeling the hot breeze sigh over my bare back as I drifted in and out of alertness. Ian's chest rose and fell as he snored flippantly.

I heard a thump, but it was probably the mail man. Ian said his landlords were away on vacation, so we had the house to ourselves. I closed my eyes again.

Then loud banging yanked her out of our stupor. Who was here?

"Someone's here!" I hissed at Ian, who had jumped from the bed, his face a deep red as he struggled to pull his pants on. Legs still wobbly, I fumbled for my clothing, which trailed from the door to the bed. I barely yanked my sweatpants over my hips when someone hit the door hard enough the wood cracked.

The banging pounded louder. "Police! Open up! We know you are in there!"

Ian froze. His face turned white as a ghost, his big, powerful body trembling. "Oh, fuck." His chin trembled.

"Ian?" I asked. My heart began to beat. "What's going on?"

He was drenched in sweat.

I turned to him desperately. "What do they want? Ian, what is this?"

The banging ended, and I heard the shuffle of booted feet on the landing outside. The male voice on the other side went from aggressive to stony and forbidding. "Last chance before we break the door down!"

Ian couldn't look at me as he yanked on his jeans. "I'm sorry. Dany, I'm so sorry." His voice was low, startled. "I didn't think this would happen."

Ian, what did you do? What did you do? I trembled, my heartbeat banged in my ears. I couldn't believe this. "What did you do?" I asked again as the door to the room smashed open right off its hinges as several officers filled the room. I screamed as I yanked the sheets over my upper body.

Ian quickly hissed, "you know nothing!"

"Brody Crane?" one of them shouted.

Ian nodded slowly.

"Put your hands where we can see them! You, Ma'am, don't move!"

I froze, trembling.

Ian slowly held up his hands. "Don't hurt her," he said. "She knows nothing."

"Ian, what's going on?" I remembered the story Ian told me about Brody, his dead best friend. His car had gone over a cliff and they never found his body. Why were they calling Ian by that name? "Please talk to me!" I begged.

"I'll go quietly. Just leave her alone. " Ian avoided my gaze.

Two officers pointed guns toward him. "On your hands and knees. Now." He complied as they twisted his arm and cuffed him.

The one in charge moved to my side, tossing me Ian's black t-shirt. "Get dressed. Move it." I hurried and retrieved the shirt. Everything was a blur—rawer and more terrifying than any nightmare.

I dressed while Ian lay on the cluttered floor in handcuffs. They were taking him. And what would happen to me? I fought the tears threatening to emerge from under my eyelids. I was so confused. What was going on?

"I'm sorry, Danyelle," he choked the words. "I'm sorry I lied."

Tears filled my eyes, but before I could answer they had brought Ian back to a sitting position.

"Brody Crane, you are under arrest for the following charges: Theft by deception, and bank fraud." He started droning off Ian's Miranda Rights while Ian stared at me with watering eyes.

"No," I whispered in a low, shaky voice. "No, there has to be some mistake."

The officer ignored me and turned to the others. "Get him up."

"I'm sorry, Dani. I love you," Ian nearly whispered.

The officer dug his fingers into his arm and led him out of the door.

I stood there, tears streaming down my face. I didn't know what to think. This had to be a big misunderstanding. "Where are you taking Ian?"

As the room began to clear, a cop loomed over me. "He'll be in a holding cell until a judge decides on bail, but I wouldn't hold my breath if I were you, Miss."

"Okay," I said quietly. "Can you tell me what's going on?"

He stared at me for a second, ignoring my question. "We need to see some ID."

"It's in my purse on the desk over there," I replied mechanically.

The officer retrieved my bag and handed it to me. I reached in and grabbed my driver's license and passed it to him. "Will Ian be all right?"

"Mr. Crane will be fine. He'll see a judge in the morning. Stay still for a moment."

I stood there and looked around. There had to be some kind of explanation for all this. Or this was some kind of nightmare I'd wake up from and we'd laugh about it. After what felt like forever passed and the officer arrived back with my identification.

"We'd like it if you came by the station for some questioning."

"Huh? About what?"

"Brody Crane."

I shook my head. "I don't know what to tell you." I bowed my head. "I'm not even sure what to believe anymore." If Ian was really Brody, then the past nine months have been nothing but a lie. How would I explain this?

"It's just a few questions, that's all."

I nodded. "All right, I said."

He handed me a card. "How about tomorrow morning at let's say 9 am."

I glanced down at it. *Officer Jerrison, ... City Police.* "Okay," I said as I rose to my feet to collect my shoes, phone, keys and bag.

Outside the house my stomach turned into knots as I slowly walked down the driveway to my car that was parked on the street. I didn't know what to think. His friend drove off a cliff he told me. Was that a lie as well? If so then who or where was the real Ian Fogg? Or was that why he didn't have a license? Or maybe this was just one big misunderstanding? Ian wouldn't do this to me. He … he couldn't!

I drove up and down the side streets, not sure what I was supposed to do. How would I explain his arrest once it hit the news to everyone? My friends, my mother, my job, everything was on the line. My reputation was at risk. A pain formed in my stomach. What about Ian's reputation? His neighbors had to have seen him hauled off in handcuffs.

I didn't want to go home yet, not with reminders of Ian all over the place. Then it thought about Waylon. Did he know about Ian? He practically treated him like as son. Maybe he was involved in this somehow? The secrets, the close friendship and the fact he had no other close friends besides me was weird. I wiped away my tears and tried to get it together. Someone needed to tell Waylon and since Ian had no one else, it would have to fall on my lap. Maybe Waylon could explain to me why the hell Ian was using someone's else identity.

I drove through the downtown core, hitting every traffic light and stop sign possible. I paid extra attention to the road. I didn't want to accidentally hurt someone or cause an accident like the day I ran into *Ian Fogg*. That name left a bitter taste in my mouth. I loved him so much but I was so damn angry at him. I felt like an idiot.

Soon I pulled into the shop parking lot of Waylon's shop. There were a few cars in the parking lot, and one garage door was up with a car about to leave. I pulled up to the front. My arms trembled a little, and my throat felt dry. How was I going to tell Waylon this especially when I didn't think he really cared for me in the first place?

Here goes nothing. I exited the car. I was a few steps away from the car before I realized I hadn't even locked it.

I entered the front door. My hands were shaky, but I prayed he was even here because I never exactly got an address for the guy's main address.

"Can I help you?" A mechanic arrived at the entrance holding a wrench.

"I'm looking for Waylon."

He glanced at the clock. "He ran out to run to grab some things. You'll have to come back later."

"I'll wait," I said without even really thinking. I turned and took a seat by the window. My body trembled and I made quick glances up at the mechanic who just stood there.

"Is there anything I could help you with?"

"You could call Waylon and tell him I need to speak him urgently, otherwise I'm staying put."

The mechanic sighed as another one came up front. "Isn't that Ian's girlfriend?" I heard one whisper to the other.

"I knew she looked familiar. I wondered where Ian was at."

My heart skipped a beat. So they didn't know yet, which meant Waylon likely didn't either.

"She is looking for Waylon, says it's important."

He sighed. "Then call him and tell him. See what he suggests we do because I heard she is stubborn."

I wanted to jump up and scream. But I forced myself to sit. I couldn't keep still. I stirred, but who could blame me.

The two mechanics left briefly. I sat alone in the entry way. Peeling paint on the walls made it look just as rundown as the outside had. I tried to reach over for something to read, or something to keep my mind off it. How could I get myself involved with someone who could lie to me? I was never going to date anyone ever again. Once my mom found out, I didn't even want to think about that.

The original mechanic arrived to the front. "He'll be back in a few minutes." He left before I could respond.

I sat there in silence when a man, who wasn't Waylon, walked in. The mechanic spoke a few words with him while the smell of diesel made me bile form in my throat. A wave of nauseous. This was the second time this week that the smell of diesel made me what to hurl. It had to be stress.

Waylon walked into the front lobby, his face contorted into a deep frown.

"Danyelle," he said in a low, rough voice.

I jumped.

"Is Ian with you?" he asked, a sense of dismay in his voice.

I shook my head and whispered, "Is there somewhere we can talk, in private?"

Waylon eyebrows drew together and he nodded. "Yes, in my office. Follow me."

I followed him through the doors, through the garage where everyone stopped to look at me. He opened the door to the office and I entered. He closed and locked the door and turned on a fan I assumed was to drain out any sound.

He turned his focus at me. "Okay, so what's up? Is Ian all right?"

I wrinkled my brow and bit my lip, before forcing myself to say. "No, he isn't all right."

Waylon shuffled from foot to foot. "Where is he?"

"He was arrested." My whole body shook uncontrollably. "For stealing someone's identity." An immense weight pounded in my chest. Just speaking those words threatened to bring me to my knees.

Waylon sat down, one hand on his head. "Shit, shit. shit." He mumbled some more colorful profanities before he stopped and looked at me. "Are you sure? Who told you this? Did Ian call you?"

I shook my head. "We were sleeping when they barged in. They called him Brody Crane. All Ian could say was sorry repeatedly. He looked scared. Like terrified." His expression was still ingrained in my mind. They dragged him out there like he was some kind of hardcore criminal. But maybe he was, why else would he steal someone's identity? But I didn't want to jump to conclusions because he was always good to me.

Waylon was as pale as a ghost, similar to how Ian had appeared.

My breath caught in my throat.

That means Waylon knew all along.

"Did you talk to the police?" he asked.

"Not yet, but I'm supposed to go in there for an interview tomorrow."

Waylon glared at me, and I took a step back toward the door. Then he started mumbling. "I told him not to get involved with anyone. I told him to keep a low profile because this would happen."

"And what difference would that have made?" I raised my voice, then lowered it, realizing anyone could have been listening. "It's not like I knew. I thought Brody Crane was his friend who drove over a cliff. But who knows how much of what he said was a lie?"

"Okay, so they haven't talked to you yet."

"How long have you known about this?" I blurted. I needed to know what he knew. About why Ian did this.

Waylon grimaced. "He had good reasons. The less you know the better."

I felt the anger build on the inside. I stood. "I'm leaving."

I turned to leave when he grabbed my shoulder. I stopped and pulled.

"Please, Danyelle, wait," Waylon said. "He needs help. He is not a bad guy. I just think the less you know the better. He wouldn't want you involved more then you already are."

"I really have nothing else to say about Ian or Brody or whoever he is."

"I know you are upset. But he isn't a bad guy. He cared about you. You're all he talked about."

I bit my lip. "Yet he lied to me. I don't know if I can do this," I said. "Is there somewhere I can drop off all his stuff he left at my house? I want to forget all about him. I should have just called the police when we met. Then I wouldn't be in this mess."

"Just promise me you won't mention that I knew. I can't help him if they know I know."

I sighed. "I won't mention this conversation. Because beside this conversation, I don't know you know. But I won't lie either." I turned my gaze away. "I really do hope he is okay. I got to go" Without another word I left.

I sat in my car filled with mixed emotions. Waylon knew all along. I had so many more questions than answers. Like did he help Ian fake his identity? Or did Ian confide in him at some point? I wanted to believe he had a good reason for all this. He was so good to me, that I couldn't picture him doing something like this without a good reason. But I couldn't help but feel fuming at how this was going to affect me.

I drove around for a bit, with the music cranked up. Because once I got home, I'd be locking myself in, because once news got out, I feared privacy as I knew it would be a thing of the past. Not to mention, how my mother would react. And how Kiera would react. She would want to know every detail and like my mom see my like an idiot.

I drove around for what felt like forever before I finally conceded and drove home. I parked my car on the next block over and hid inside my house in time for the six o'clock news. Soon the whole country will know the truth. I'd be walking around with those pity stares. How could she not know? Or the rumors of, she was harboring a fugitive. How could I face the world again? I lay under the covers, with my phone on silent waiting for the flood of calls that would surely come my way.

Mom liked Ian. She thought he was a gentleman, sweet as pie and a perfect match. How would she take it he was nothing but a fraud? What would she think of me? I made no mistakes; I was so careful, so perfect. But that image would be shattered. I hugged my pillow.

There was a knock on the door but I didn't answer it. I didn't log on to any social media. I was closing myself off from the world. Tomorrow I had to call in sick to work to go talk to the police, and I wasn't sure how I would get out of my house unseen. I thought about going out the back, through the back gate, and down the back alley to my car, but that in itself seemed foolish. I shouldn't feel ashamed for being lied too. There was no way I'd known that he wasn't who he said he was.

Unable to relax I got out of bed, restless. I picked up Ian's clothes he had scattered among every square inch of the room and tossed it on the bed. A part of me wanted to erase every trace he even stepped foot in my house. But I couldn't. Not without hearing his side of the story.

***

The following morning my alarm went off at eight. I woke up groggy. There were over a dozen missed calls from my mother, and from Kiera. I didn't want to deal with any of them right now. Instead I took the time to text my boss telling him I was sick and wouldn't be in. I couldn't even care about his reaction at this time.

I had to get it together to go talk to the police. The very people who arrested him. I got dressed. Out front was my mom's SUV, out front. There wasn't anyone else. My guess they were swarming in front of Ian's house. I had read the headlines from five thirty five on. *Brody Crane was arrested for identity theft.* I threw my hair into a ponytail, and without thinking put one of Ian's t-shirts on.

I went out the back door to avoid my mother as I headed for my vehicle.

When I got into the car, I found myself naturally driving toward the police station. I wondered how he was doing. His expression was still embedded in my mind. He kept saying he was sorry over and over again.

I parked a block from the station and sat there. I still had a few minutes before I had to go in. Maybe they could explain to me what the hell was going on. And I wasn't a criminal and had nothing to hide.

I got out of my car, smoothed out the front of Ian's t-shirt and walked up the steep concrete pathway to the front doors. I swallowed hard as I walked into the police station. I approached the front desk.

"May I help you?" a female officer asked.

"I have an appointment with Officer Jerrison," I said meekly.

"And your name?"

"Danyelle Fitzgerald."

Without making eye contact she said, "Take a seat. I'll let him know you're here."

I nodded and offered a weak, "Okay."

I plopped down on the hard bench. I crossed and uncrossed my arms. I didn't know what to think. Did they think I knew about his true identity? And would they expect me to throw him under the bus. I glanced at my phone, as a few minutes passed the allotted meeting time. People kept walking back and forth. There was chit chat in one corner about lunch. How could they act so normal?

"Danyelle."

I jumped and looked up at the desk "Yeah?"

"He's ready for you."

I clasped on to my bag as I followed her behind the desk to a semi lit room, with a glass window, and a metal table and two chairs. It had a cold aura to it, and I felt a chill shoot up my back. I wondered if I should have maybe hired a lawyer. But at the same time, I didn't do anything wrong. I was that good girl.

I took a seat while the other officer sat down. "Thanks for coming in," he said warmly.

"Okay." I wanted to say that it felt like I didn't have a choice but I kept my mouth shut.

"Can I get you anything? Coffee, water?"

"No thanks," I replied, fiddling with my purse for a few seconds.

"I know this is unexpected and the circumstances aren't great, but I'd like to ask you a couple questions about Brody Crane."

I opened my mouth to speak and stared at the officer as tears once again tried to emerge. "I've always known him as Ian." I sat here, the denial started to wane. It was hard to comprehend, and a part of me, the subconscious part of me, said that this would all be one big joke. I'd be so mad at Ian later for doing this to me, and we could laugh it off.

He took a paper out of the folder and showed it to me. It had the address blacked out, but it was a photocopy of an Alaska driver's license with a picture of Ian with the name Brody Crane.

"I know this is hard to take in but I need a few answers."

I blinked away the tears. "Okay. I'll help you in any way I can."

"First of all, how did you two meet?"

My stomach coiled as the moment where we first met came flashing back. "We met when I crashed my car into him. He said he didn't have insurance, so we made a deal, and he paid to have my car fixed."

The officer jotted it down. I felt suddenly sick to my stomach. I was admitting to a police officer that I knew that he was breaking the law, even as minor as driving without insurance and didn't say anything. In the grand scheme of things, I guess it was pretty minor compared to ... well, whatever Ian had done.

"Have you ever heard of Brody Crane before?"

I stirred in my chair. I hated talking about him this way even though he lied to me. "I was under the impression his friend's name was Brody, and that he drove over the cliff and they never recovered his body. The thing is he sounded so upset about it. He told me he was his best friend. But now I wonder if all he told me was just a lie." I sighed and buried my hands in my face for a moment.

The officer nodded. "What else did he tell you?"

"He told me that Brody's family didn't care about him. He said that there wasn't one interview or anything of is family begging for his safe return." The tears flowed. "He was so broken up over it. Ian said he felt bad because he never gotten a proper burial."

"About Ian or do you mean Brody?" the officer inquired.

"He referred to his friend as Brody. I've always known him as Ian. So tell me was there ever an accident or was that a lie?"

The officer didn't say anything at first.

"I just want to know what the hell is going on," I stuttered, trying to be strong. "I feel like the last nine months have been one big lie. There has to be some truth to his words. Ian, or Brody, or whatever his real name is, wasn't a bad guy. Not the guy I knew, or thought I knew, anyway."

I was so confused. Was Ian just one big lie? "I know this is difficult for you."

I wanted to scream, *no you don't. He had no idea how difficult this was for me.* "I just want to know what he was running from!"

I realized I was talking more then I should. I needed to keep it together, because the police was looking for anything they could to nail to Ian.

"Is there anything else he told you? Anything about his past? Anything? We can't help him if we don't know the truth."

"He said his parents were dead, and they were addicts. But beside that he didn't really say anything. He was pretty closed off."

"How about violent? Was he ever violent or shown violent tendencies?" Yelling, screaming, that sort of thing?"

That question caught me off guard. "No. I can't even really recall him ever yelling as long as I've known him. He was distant and guarded but definitely not violent."

The officer then switched to questions about what else he told me. I answered each question as truthfully as I could. I felt so conflicted, so confused. He told me so much about Brody and now I wonder if it was the truth. Was he talking about himself this entire time? Because he showed so much emotion.

Finally the questioning ended, and the police officer said we'd be in touch. I got up to leave but stopped. "Is he okay? Like really? I know you don't care about him, but I do."

The officer sported a crooked, half-hearted smile. "I'm sure he's fine. Thanks again for coming in. Have a good afternoon, Ms. Fitzgerald. "
I left the police station deflated. What did this mean for us? Would I ever see him again? I sat in my car and sighed.

13

Mom had been blowing up my phone, and I had been locking myself away from everyone. What would I possibly say to her? How could I look her in the face? She loved Ian. She loved him, and I let that expectation down. She trusted my judgement, but I let my guard down and look what happened. Worst part was all the warning signs had hit me in the face like a ton of bricks.

Who is Ian really? Why was he going by a different name? Please answer me, sweetie.

She was so calm, and that was what scared me.

I know you are home. So don't ignore me, Danyelle.

What should I tell her? What explanation could I give her when I didn't even know what the hell was going on? It was hard to believe a little less than forty-eight hours ago I had discovered the truth. I wiped sweat from my forehead and paced. What else could I do? I couldn't face my family. I couldn't even walk out my front door without risking a reporter or someone demanding answers I didn't have.

My stomach tingled as tears rose behind my eyelids. I couldn't shed anymore tears nor could I calm this nagging, sick feeling in my gut. That was what I got when I ignored my intuition. Ian was too good to be true.

He conned me.

He lied to me.

Why didn't I just call the police when he didn't have insurance? I should have known then and there. I should have known he was hiding something more sinister when I had to beg him and basically drag any truth out of him.

Then I remembered the photo. The photo with who I thought was his friend Brody. Was that the real Ian? I still remembered his face in the picture. He had a sadness to him. I had to wonder if that was true? Did his friend actually drive over the edge? Or… I shook my head, trying to remove those thoughts. Ian wasn't a bad guy. Waylon said so. I had to believe it--at least, I wanted to. I had to believe it because I could be wrong, because the assumption that he may have had done something to the real Ian was too much.

The doorbell rang, and I jumped. I quietly looked through the peep hole. It was Kiera along with my mother. Shit! Shit! Shit! What did she tell my mom? Mom would be even angrier once she found out I lied to her about how I met Ian. She would for sure think I was imprudent. I'd be that naïve daughter. I'd be an embarrassment.

I took a deep breath, crouched down in front of the door and buried my head in my hands. The knocking grew louder. My phone in my pocket kept ringing. I was trapped, and the only way out was to confront them.

I stood, one hand on the doorknob, and opened the door.

Mom pushed her way through, and Kiera followed. "It's about time you answered the door."

I didn't respond. I felt my face turn hot. The whole world felt like it was caving in. Mom stood akimbo, her lips pinched together. "Well?"

Kiera took a deep, labored breath. "You weren't answering your phone so we came over here."

I shifted from foot to foot. What was I going to say? "I'm fine." I said, trying to convince both them and myself. Only I wasn't fine. Everything was just so overwhelming.

There was a brief moment of silence.

"How long did you know his real name wasn't Ian?" Kiera asked.

I turned and stared at Mom, who clenched her jaw. They both were teaming up on me in my own house.

"Two days ago," I whispered. "I had no idea..." I mumbled something to myself. I had no idea. I felt so stupid, so small.

Mom cursed under her breath. "How could you not know, Danyelle? There are always warning signs. Like him keeping secrets. You should have been able to spot them, Dany. Do you know what people are saying?" The frown lines on her forehead intensified.

Ian was a good actor, so I wasn't the only one he fooled. "You liked him, so you obviously didn't notice anything amiss either!" I shot back.

"I liked him because you have always had good judgement. But it's clear, Danyelle. You have let your father and me down greatly. We are so disappointed. The question is what are we going to do about this mess? Do you have a plan? A course of action?"

I tensed up. It felt like a punch to the gut.

"Well, Danyelle? What are you going to do about it? How do you suppose we explain this to all of our friends? How do we look at people and explain that our daughter, the one who had everything going for her, all the potential in the world, the one who had good morals and good judgement, could allow a fraud into her life, into our family?"

"He isn't a bad guy!" I found myself blurting out, and I realized just how ridiculous I sounded.

Kiera rolled her eyes.

I glared at her.

"What?" she asked smugly.

"Well, he wasn't a bad guy. At least I didn't think so."

Kiera sighed. "You knew from the beginning that he wasn't responsible. You took a risk, and obviously it didn't work out for you."

A sheen of sweat formed on my cheeks, chin, and forehead. "You are the one who set us up to fucking date in the first place." Why the hell was she bringing this up now of all times--and in front of my mother?

Kiera sneered. "Don't blame me." She flicked her hair above her shoulder. "You said you liked him, so I helped you out."

"No one asked you." I flapped my hands and growled. "Why are you even here?" I mumbled.

Why was either one of them here?

"What does she mean he was irresponsible?" Mom asked.

"Nothing..." I began to pace. "It doesn't matter."

I just wanted them both to go. I wanted them to both just leave me alone. I felt a wave of nausea overcome me. I blew out a series of short breaths. "I need to lay down." My words were weak. My heart sped up as my anxiety crept up again.

"Will someone tell me what the hell is going on? What else has Ian, or whoever this fraud is, has done?" Mom let out a long, exasperated breath. "I'm so disappointed in you. You have obviously done wrong. You can't even be honest with me!"

I clenched my fist. "Fine!" I shouted. "I crashed into him. He didn't have insurance. Instead of calling the police, he fixed my car, even though I was at fault. Then after that we started dating. There. Is there anything else you want to know? Or are you going to keep telling me you are disappointed in me?" I took several deep breaths, trying to keep my composure. "I had no idea he wasn't who he said he was. Sure, he was a little closed off, but I wanted to give him the benefit of the doubt, because he had so many other great qualities. So will you just stop?"

Mom wasn't fazed. "So what other lies has he told you? Is he even a real plumber? Or is that made up? Or is he even from Alaska? Tell me? What do you really know about him?"

I paced. What did I know about him? He had lied to me. He wasn't who he said he was. But I loved him. Or who I thought he was. "What I do know is he was loving. He was nice to me and would give the shirt on his back to anyone. That is what I know about him."

A wave of emotion overcame me. On one hand I was so angry with him, but on the other hand my heart was split in two. Was he still the same person? Just using someone else's name? He was handsome, charming, witty and more. He was there for me. We had so much chemistry. I wasn't sure if I was ready to let him go. But what choice did I have? He was arrested, and for all I knew, he would be sent back to Alaska or wherever he came from.

Mom shook her head and walked past Kiera and me. "I can't do this, Danyelle. I have never been so disappointed in one of my children in all my life. I have nothing else to say to you."

Without another word, she exited through my front door.

I stood there without a word and peeked through the cracks. There was a news truck across the street. Mom paid no attention as she sped off.

I sat on the couch and sighed. I pressed my lips together into a slight grimace.

Kiera rubbed the back of her neck. "Sorry, Dany. I didn't expect for her to react that way."

I glared at her and said nothing. What was the point? She knew very well how my mom was going to react. The question was why she dragged her around.

She exhaled. "Will you talk to me?"

She sat down beside me, inches away. I took a whiff of her overpowering perfume, and thick bile formed in my throat. The sickly feeling rose. I turned my head slightly away.

Kiera frowned. "Why are you treating me like this? I only brought your mom because we were both worried about you."

I opened my mouth to say something I shouldn't, but I stopped myself. "This hasn't been easy for me."

Kiera rose and headed for my kitchen, and I followed. She opened my fridge and helped herself to some soda. "Of course it isn't easy. No one said it was. But still you should have known."

Should've, could've, would've. It didn't matter. I couldn't change the fact that I made a mistake thanks to my poor judgment.

"How does one know?" I asked her. "He was closed off, and now I understand why. Like, who would expect someone would be using a fake name? One would expect something shady like living a double life or stealing a car when they were twenty. Right? I used bad judgment. That I did."

Kiera took a deep breath. "We all make mistakes, hun. But this one was a doozy. And I thought *my* relationships were bad."

I stared at her as if I was shooting daggers from my eyes. "Ian…I mean Brody…wasn't an abusive asshole!" I flinched. Without even realizing it, I was defending Ian.

"Pft." Kiera glanced away. "At least he wasn't using someone else's identity. And besides, why are you even defending him? Look what he has done to you, to your family! How do you think your parents are feeling?"

I gazed downward, struggling to find the right words to describe how I was feeling. "What about how I feel?"

If there was one thing Ian taught me, it was to stop worrying about what others thought. I had spent so much time worrying that I put up a façade instead of just being myself. That was another thing that made this so hard. He brought out my best qualities. He challenged me and supported me.

Kiera rolled her eyes. "What you need to do is: pack up whatever shit he left here, load it up into your car, and dump it. Then come back here, get dressed up, go out, and get laid. We can go to the next town over. You can use an alias and forget about him. You can deal with this mess tomorrow."

She paused. "After you sleep off the hangover you're going to get."

"I'm not going anywhere."

Kiera's face turned a deep crimson. "Fine, stay here, and wallow in your self-pity! I tried. I really did."

"Maybe I'll do that!" I spat back.

"Whatever. Deal with this on your own." She got up, headed through the kitchen, and left out my front door just as my mom had. I locked the door behind her and sank to the ground.

What was I going to do? I couldn't hide forever. Sooner or later, I'd have to go out there. I had to accept that Ian wasn't who he said he was. I had to accept that my parents, especially my mother, weren't ever going to look at me the same way again.

I grabbed my phone and headed upstairs to my bedroom. It was only noon, and this would be the second day I called out of work. So far, no one had said anything, but I knew my boss didn't like it when I missed multiple days in a row. Whether I liked it or not, I would have to go in tomorrow.

I went online and typed in "Brody Crane," hoping for some kind of update. There was an article from ten minutes ago. The headline read: *Co-Worker Speaks Out about Ian Fogg aka Brody Crane.*

My curiosity piqued, and I opened the link.

It started off with a summary of what I already knew, followed by a picture of a man with greasy hair, dressed in a baggy T-shirt embroidered with the logo of Ian's former employer.

We have spoken with Matthew Dawson, the co-worker of Brody Cane (formally known as Ian Fogg). Dawson said: "Ian was a cool guy. You could count on him. He worked hard. But on the other hand, he was kind of closed off. He'd joke around, but outside of work he kept to himself. I don't believe he had many friends. Nevertheless, I'm shocked. I really am. We all are."

So, he was liked among his co-workers, or one at least. I couldn't wrap my head around it. Why? Why was he using someone else's identity? What was he so afraid of? I wished Waylon had told me something, anything. He said it was better if I didn't know. I understood he was protecting Ian — or Brody. I didn't know if I could get used to calling him that. It just didn't fit him.

I grabbed one of his sweatshirts that hung off the nearby end table and hugged it. I swore it smelt like him, even if it was just in my head. I found myself dozing off. It was much welcomed. I had barely slept since all this shit hit the fan. Then all of a sudden, my phone vibrated, and my eyes shot open.

A text. I had been receiving a lot of those lately. But I doubt it was Mom. She likely wouldn't try to contact me for a few days at least. Maybe Kiera? I sighed. Who I really wanted it to be was behind bars.

I opened it. It was a text from my boss. My jaw dropped...

Danyelle. I know you are going through a hard time. I watched the news and thought about it very hard. This isn't personal, but I'm afraid I have to let you go, effective immediately.

I stared at the message, and my mind went numb. I was at a loss for words. Fired? I had never been fired from anything in all my life. I never failed. I was a straight A student, and I succeeded at everything I did. There was an immense weight on my shoulders. *Failure.* I couldn't get that out of my head. How could I lose my job?

I ground my teeth together and clenched my phone in my hand. My knuckles turned white, and my chest constricted. What was I going to do? Heat flashed through my body, and my heart pounded. I chucked my phone as hard as I could, and it bounced off the wall on to the floor. I crumbled to my hands and knees and let it all out.

14

A week passed before I was able to move my car back into my driveway. For the first time in days, I finally felt like I could breathe. Mom and Kiera hadn't attempted to text me and the random phone calls and texts had stopped, and the outside media had moved on to other stories.

But my life was still problematic. I was basically housebound with my last paycheck dwindling. There was still my savings, which was of course for an emergency. Well, this could define as an emergency, but not the kind I was hoping for.

What I needed was a job. There were no more museums hiring. My whole life was turned upside down. I loved my job. It was easy, I enjoyed the culture and the customers. It weighed on me. My fists clenched. IT was just another shit sandwich I was forced to swallow. I had a few clients' jobs I had to finish up this week but nothing substantial. Nothing but my four months' worth of savings, which if I didn't find something quick I'd diminish through. God forbid if my furnace or something else broke. I didn't want to think about it. With how my life was going something bad would happen, I knew it.

I struggled for most of the day with a tightness building in my chest. All morning I spent updating my resume and the few clients and co-workers I texted hadn't agreed to let me use them as a reference. I sighed. They probably didn't want to be associated with someone like me who knew Ian Fogg. I clenched my jaw. I wished I never met Ian. This nightmare was all his fault. Why did I have to be at that intersection? If I had never trusted him and just turned him in in the first place I'd never be in this situation. The deductible would have been a lot less painful than all of this.

I looked through the job listings. I had a degree in history but nothing that would make a difference. Would I be stuck making minimum wage? I sighed and wiped dots of sweat from my forehead. I didn't make loads of money at the gift shop but at least I made enough to live on. How could I survive making under ten dollars an hour? I exhaled vociferously. Maybe I could apply for a supervisor or something. Like get out of my comfort zone, out of the field of interest all together. But who was I kidding – I had almost no supervisor skills. I was a cashier, a history tour guide and seamstress. I didn't know the first thing about being a manager.

I scoped out and applied to fourteen different positions, ranging from supervisor to a hair salon, and even a receptionist to a hotel. Basically, anything over eleven dollars an hour. I just hoped I wouldn't need to lower my standards. That'd just add to the disdain my family already felt about me. A cold shiver pierced me from head to toe and down my back.

I needed a break. My stomach grumbled. I realized I hadn't eaten all day. I checked my bank account to see if I could squeeze a few dollars for something to eat. It was warm outside, I was sick to my stomach from stress and I was craving something spicy. Yes, something hot and exotic. But why? I wasn't big on spicy things, like ever. But I was known to have the odd craving here and there. I groaned at the total, but right now I didn't care. I needed comfort food and I needed to eat.

I called and ordered myself some red curry chicken on rice from the Thai place down the road. It was random, but it would be just what I needed to distract me from my stressful life.

I paced the room, my palms sweating and my hands trembling. What was I doing? I shouldn't be ordering take out around a time like this. A time where I have little income coming in. Beside the few outgoing jobs I had, it wasn't stable. Perspiration dotted my forehead as the guilt washed over me. My impulsive decisions were going to do me in. I clasped my hands to my chest and breathed in and out. It was a one-time thing. I wouldn't order anymore take out. Not until I had a new job and this whole mess with Ian was behind me.

Just the thought of Ian almost brought me to my knees. I couldn't stop thinking about him and every attempt of forgetting about him, whether it's thinking of food, a new job, or some random history documentary, which I hadn't had the luxury to really sit and enjoy, had failed me.

I entered the living room and paced some more, making glances out the window for my food. I was starving now. Five, ten, and finally fifteen minutes passed until a white older style sedan pulled up. My insides temporary pulled in every direction. It was just the delivery driver, I told myself. But what it really was, was really just another reminder of Ian. I wanted nothing more than to go back to almost ten days ago, before the truth came out, and stare into his racing eyes and feel his touch.

The doorbell rang and that image wiped away. I headed with an obvious bounce to my step to the front door to grab my order. I paid, even giving a tip before closing the door. If I didn't tip that guilt would etch into my mind but I felt shitty because I didn't have a job, so tipping should have been the last thing I did. But again, I shouldn't have bought this damn food in the first place.

I sat on the couch and opened the brown paper bag and pulled out the Styrofoam takeout container. The curry seeped into my senses and the bile in the back of my throat rose. I stumbled backward, holding my stomach with the sudden queasiness that washed over me.

I threw the container down and ran for the bathroom. I hovered over the toilet and heaved. My heart sped up, and my face flushed. I plopped down on the ground next to the toilet and tried to control my rapid breaths. The smell of curry still lingered. It made me feel sick all over again.

I'm okay, I told myself. The stress was getting to me, and if I were to feel any worse I wouldn't be able to go to the doctor because as of today I had no insurance. But the stress and lack of sleep was catching up to me. *That's it,* I tried to convince myself. *I just need sleep.*

But I glanced up at the top shelf, at the box of tampons that had split over, and a few were hanging down. Then the painful realization dawned on me.

I couldn't remember the last time I had my period.

No! No! No! It couldn't be.

I buried my face in my hands. Ian and I were careful most of the time, but a few times we weren't. I groaned and bit my upper lip as I fidgeted with my collar. It was all in my head, it had to be. I was just stressed. I had no job. The odd time we didn't, surely couldn't have cause this.

I got off the floor, and smoothed out my blouse. I was going to drive myself crazy. I wasn't pregnant. I couldn't be. I recalled back to the hours of internet searches back to my last pregnancy scare. Stress could cause a delayed period and make one feel nauseous, right?

That was it. I ambled back to the living room and paced. It was likely all in my head but I needed to know for sure if I was. Otherwise it'd eat at me. I retrieved my keys and left, leaving the take out still on the coffee table. My stomach grumbled but I couldn't eat it anyway.

I arrived at the drug store, still in my pajama pants and hair disheveled. I didn't care. I glanced around to see if I knew anyone. I didn't need it to get out that I was buying a pregnancy test so soon after my boyfriend or ex-boyfriend was discovered to be a swindle.

I found the family planning aisle. Ironic it was named that, because having a baby and a family was the last thing on my mind. I grabbed a few dollar brands, and one of those digitals. I would have bought more if I had extra money lying around.

I took the quickest route to the till, and an older woman I haven't seen before rang my order. I took some side glances out toward the street and so far my luck had been good. I hadn't' seen anyone who would potentially give a shit about my predicament.

"That'll be twelve thirty-three, please," the lady said.

I jumped and pulled out my credit card.

"Have a good day," she said in an equally low, monotone voice before scanning the stuff of the person behind me.

I hurried for my car, hoping, praying no one saw me. This nightmare couldn't get any worse… Or it could, but I was convinced that wasn't going to happen.

No sooner then I was in the drive way, I grabbed the bag and ran in the front door, then turned and locked the door.

I paced a few times. Maybe I'll take the cheap test first. But then I looked at the digital. It'd give me a clear positive or negative answer, because honestly I needed to know and didn't want any guess work. Sweat drenched me from head to toe. God, please…

I guzzled down a glass of water.

And waited. And waited some more.

I paced some more. It was almost an hour before I had a bladder full enough. I had waited extra for good measure, so the test wouldn't be watered down. I read somewhere that it could cause a false positive. But, maybe deep down inside I just didn't want to know the results. I have put myself into this self-contained bubble; others called in denial.

I opened the test inside the bathroom and a few minutes later, set it on the counter, then paced in and out of the bathroom for the next three minutes. All awhile waiting, praying, hoping for a negative.

I picked up the test and gasped.

Pregnant.

I set it back on the sink ledge and walked out of the bathroom.

In the hallway and I took a step forward and two steps back, in no particular rhythm. I covered my mouth with my sweaty palm. Positive. It was clear of day. There was no line to dissect.. It was clear as day. Pregnant. My gaze wandered at nothing in particular. What was I going to do? I couldn't be pregnant. Could I? I stared back at the bathroom door at the test on the ledge. I couldn't believe it, but the proof was there. I was always one to need proof to convince myself, but as of late, even with proof I was denying it.

What was I going to do? I rubbed my forehead and shook my head. I had no job and Ian, Brody, or whoever he was, the father was in jail, and probably being extradited back to Alaska. Mom would freak, and Kiera wouldn't understand. Ian had no family that I knew of. I would be in this all on my own.

I'd have no one.

I couldn't do this.

I couldn't have this baby.

Then I remembered the clinic. I remember when I called them to make an appointment, that they had walk in appointments from four to six. Glancing at the clock, I realized I had enough time to get there. I remember they also offered a pill that could get rid of this pregnancy. The pit in my stomach intensified. I felt like such a shitty person for even considering this, but what choice did I have?

But I couldn't be pregnant. I couldn't be constantly reminded of the man who lied to me, and turned my life upside down. Not to mention Ian was in no position to help support a baby.

I hurried to the bedroom to get dressed. I needed to make it to the clinic before it closed for the day. This would be the last poor decision I made. I swore going forward I'd up my expectations. I'd go back to be that girl who didn't take risks, who didn't give people the benefit of the doubt. I'd get a new job, and all of this would blow over. I'd show my parents that I am still that good girl. That this was a onetime mistake, never to be repeated.

I arrived at the clinic, in tears. Half nervous, half relieved but most of all guilty. I never expected I'd find myself in this predicament, especially after the last pregnancy scare. Lingering feelings from New Year's Eve was still on my mind. I had sorta pushed it to the back burner and the only person I had told was the one who stabbed me in the back the most.

I walked up to the receptionist and gave her my name and told her what I was there for.

"Please take a seat," she said.

I walked and sat down on those same worn chairs, and picked up one of the same magazines I skimmed nine months earlier. It was so ironic being here for this reason. I was so judgmental being here before. I was cynical, like someone with something shoved up their butt. But now, in comparison I was jaded. I was scared. I thought meeting Ian would have changed my life; I thought I met the one. Now I was pregnant with that same man's baby.

Why was this so hard? I was so consumed with what he had done, yet at times I was defending him. I knew deep in my heart Ian wasn't a bad guy. He was kind and made me laugh. He was attractive, responsible for the most part, and kept his word. Here I was sitting here, making a decision that would affect him, even if he never found out. I knew. I knew that I was keeping a secret from him, like he had me.

I grimaced as names were called one after another. Soon it would be my turn. Soon I'd be ending the last tie I had to Ian. But the truth was I wasn't sure if I could go through with it. My leg bounced, and I broke out in a sweat.

"Danyelle Fitzgerald," the medical nurse called.

I jumped up. Here goes nothing, I thought as I followed her through the doors to what would be the biggest decision I ever made.

15

I couldn't go through with it. They confirmed the pregnancy through blood testing, and when I went back to the clinic today to take the pill to end the pregnancy, I couldn't do it. All the previous night I tossed and turned, waking up in cold sweats, and immense guilt weighed down on me. Ultimately, I never showed up.

There were two voicemails from the clinic, after I let both phone calls go to voicemail. After the first message, I deleted them. No, I didn't want to reschedule. Both choices weren't great. This was a situation I never thought I'd find myself in. This whole year had been a yo-yo of events I wished I could take back, even the good memories. It was the year as a whole. It was the worst year of my life. I lost so much, that I couldn't let myself lose another thing. So, I changed my mind, and decided to keep the baby. To not end the pregnancy. This was the one thing right now I could control, and I didn't want to be responsible or that person.

I rubbed my stomach, the hard-cold truth of the situation weighing on my mind. The father of this baby was another mystery, but I couldn't get him out of head, my heart. Was this pregnancy a sign? I didn't believe in symbolism or fate, but if there was such a thing then this was it.

I hadn't taken the time to really verify anything Ian said. I remember back to the photo of Ian and his friend. The real Ian. I wondered if the truth about him going over the cliff and his body never being found until recently was true.

I closed the curtains in the living room and retrieved my laptop from the end table which was in a great need of dusting. I slouched into the couch, kicking my legs up on the equally dusty coffee table, and propped the laptop on my lap.

I typed Brody Crane into the search engine. I scrolled through the headlines for anything that didn't indicate what I already knew which was Ian was a fraud. I wanted a why. What was he scared of, what was he hiding and why. That question I tried to push to the back of my mind because I was so sure I wanted to push Ian to the past. But now that wasn't possible. I couldn't go through with terminating the pregnancy. How much I tried, but I couldn't do it. It was a decision I'd have to own, including all the backlash that came along with it.

I kept scrolling when I came across a headline "Ian Fogg identified as man found deceased in Northern Alaska."

I clicked the link, and scrolled through the story when I stopped at a section of interest.

On January 14 2010, at 11:23 am we located the car belonging to Brody Crane submerged. After multiple searches of the immediate area no signs of a body could be found and he was presumed drowned. On February 15 2019, the skeleton remains of a male were located thirteen kilometers north of Mr. Cranes abandoned car nine years earlier.

Goosebumps littered both of my arms and legs. So there really was an accident. So, he wasn't lying about that.

An autopsy was performed on February 18 2019 and DNA didn't match Brody Crane. His cause of death was undetermined.

I guess there was only so much information one could get from a body that had been missing for that long. This case was never international news so Ian was right when he said that no one cared.

I set the laptop down beside me, got up and paced. Ian came from a community and based from this article, it was a small community, likely with little to no resources. But a man goes missing, is presumed dead, then a body they think is said missing man, is actually not. How could that not be top news. I watch the news and I scroll through social media and there hasn't been one article, of anything about Alaska. Also, what were they doing from February to now, which was basically the entire length of Ian and my relationship to date. Surely it couldn't be that hard to figure out who the body belonged too. Once they realized it was the real Ian Fogg, realizing that Ian's best friend went missing mysteriously around the same time he went over the edge.

But then again Ian had been living with this identity for a while. They could have pulled up tax records and realized that Ian had simply moved on. They had no reason, at least until they identified the remains to suspect anything.

So how did they find out? How did they find out Ian's really identity? He had told me he had no family. So, if the real Ian had no family, then how did they find out his true identity? There was so many questions with no answers. Why did Ian pass himself off as his best friend? What happened where he grew up that would force him to take another's identity and move across the country.

I crumpled to the floor. I couldn't come up with a single answer. I hugged myself as I let out a long drawn out sigh. He was so nice, so understanding and so funny. We had so much fun together, but he had always been closed off. Anything I learned from him was forced. And how did Waylon fit in all this, and how did he get mixed up in this whole mess with Ian.

The night before he was arrested crossed my mind. We were driving around the downtown core for something to do. We were joking and Ian mentioned taking a vacation. When I asked where he said anywhere. He smiled. He seemed so happy, and so carefree. We were heading toward our first year together. We had grown so close, and were planning for the future.

We were almost inseparable, almost overnight it seemed. But it made me wonder if he had secretly feared they were coming for him, and he wanted to flee before they could arrest him. I shook my head at that thought. Ian wouldn't do that. He wouldn't purposely take me on the run, unknowingly if he knew he was running from the police."

I wonder if Waylon was from Alaska. Both Ian and Waylon said they met when they got to this city, but with how many lies Ian had told, I bet anything Waylon knew a lot more then he was leading on, and I suspect he likely helped him across the country. Alaska was on the border of Canada, so there was only a few ways out of Alaska, one being through Canada which would have required a passport, another flying, and he would need ID for that, and or by boat, but by that time of year it would be cold.

It was obvious he had ID when he reached this state. Ian was smart, and planned his escape from Alaska very well. He was able to live under this name for nine years. But still someone had to help him pull it off. The only person I could think of was Waylon.

I pinched my lips together and placed my arms behind my back. He expected me to keep his involvement a secret buthe was hiding something from me. I wanted to march over there and demand some answers. I had a baby to think about and Ian deserved to know about this pregnancy, just as much as I deserved to know the truth.

My one hand reached, and rubbed the back of my neck. I breathed in and out, in and out, a couple times to calm my raging nerves. Every thought, scenario, ran through my mind. In thirty seconds flat I went from caring about Ian and the truth, to trying to make sense of all this.

I couldn't sit here and think about this anymore. I needed answers, and the only person who could give them to me wasn't going to make it easy.

Then maybe I could write to Ian, and tell him about the pregnancy then, and that I forgave him. Forgiveness a huge leap for me. I forgave no one except Kiera once or twice, but she was different. She was my best friend forever. But right now even we weren't talking, and it made me sad.

I needed to tell someone I was pregnant, and really the only person I could tell was Ian. I swore at myself, knowing I needed to learn to refer to him by his given name. Brody. I was never going to get used to that name.

I left the house, and got into my car. I hoped that Waylon was still at his shop. But I couldn't sit around any longer. I needed to know what was going on. I needed to know why. Why Ian did what he did.

I opted for the freeway, the same route Ian took me on the first time he took me to the shop. The familiarity bough a sense of warmth and pain at the same time. I couldn't even comprehend it. I pulled off the freeway, and down a back road before turning. I reached my destination. A bittersweet feeling emerged in my throat. I swallowed before I headed inside.

The same mechanic as the last time I showed up here approached. "You shouldn't be here," he whispered in a small voice.

I rolled my eyes. "Well, that's too bad. So why don't you go back and get Waylon." I didn't even know where my abrasiveness came from. I guess my stance was hardening again.

He mumbled something before going into the shop to get Waylon. Moments later he showed up at the door.

He swallowed hard and invited me back to his office.

"I didn't think I'd see you here again. Did the police talk to you again?"

I shook my head. "No."

Waylon ran his hand through his hair and sighed. "So, what can I do for you Danyelle?"

"I want to know what is going on with Ian."

Waylon waved his hands dismissively. "He's fine. I'm handling it."

I moved closer into his personal space. "That is not what I asked you. I want to know what is going on with Ian." I waited for a minute for a response but didn't get one. "Well?"

Waylon smirked. "Ian said you were blunt. I just never saw it. Well until now."

I burrowed a brow, my jaw set. "I'm not leaving until you tell me the truth about Ian. Like how did you find out about his true identity."

Waylon walked over to the door and locked it. "Keep it down."

I pressed my lips together. I was so sick of people telling me what I need to know, how I was supposed to feel and what I was supposed to do. I was going to regain control of things, and it started right now.

"I mean either you tell me or I'll find out on my own."

"Is that a threat?" Waylon asked with a stiff upper lip. "Because if you think you can come into my shop and…"

"It's on a threat If you take it as one. I want to know what Ian was hiding, and I rather you just tell me rather than me having to go digging." I purposely eased up a bit, hoping he'd volunteer up something I could work with.

"So why the change in attitude? Last time you were here you wanted nothing to do with him."

His question caught me off guard. I didn't want to tell him about being pregnant or that I still loved him.

"I just changed my mind. Now tell me what is going on with Ian."

Waylon paced a bit. "He had a hearing and was sent back to Alaska for prosecution. It's sad because it was the last place on this planet he wanted to return too."

"Why?"

"There was a lot of bad blood in Alaska. I don't even know all the details myself Danyelle. I befriended him shortly after his close friend drove off the cliff. I figure you know all that all ready. But he was depressed and had enough. So, I helped him out."

I bit my upper lip. "Helped how?"

Waylon sighed. "I already said too much. All I can tell you is, I helped him out of that place. I even relocated to this city to give him a helping hand. He's like a son to me…" Waylon voice trailed off. "I feared the day his true identity was revealed. I prepared him for the day. I also told him to not let anyone close."

This lit something in me. "So, you expected him to not be involved in a romantic relationship or have any close friends?"

Waylon frowned. "You don't understand, Dany." His voice was curt, and the frowns in his forehead intensified. "When I helped him out, and when he chose to take on this new alias, I made it clear he couldn't get close to anyone. He had to keep the down low, pay his taxes, work steadily and stay out of trouble. Because at anytime the truth could come out. The last thing I wanted was for you or anyone else to get involved." Waylon lowered his gaze. "He's heartbroken. I haven't talked to him directly but his lawyer who had the courtesy to call me, said he is sad, and that he never meant for any of this to happen."

"So, he wasn't allowed any visitors at all?" I asked.

"Not until he is transferred back to Alaska. It's sad because I doubt his parents will want to see him and he didn't have any friends there."

My mind spun around and around like race car on a track. So at least it was confirmed he had parents, and that Waylon helped him. But how? How did Waylon help him? It still didn't explain why Waylon would uproot his entire life, risk his freedom to help Ian across the country without another motive.

"Will he be allowed visitors in Alaska. I just hate for him to think no one cares."

"He should be back in Alaska early next week, and then I'm flying out there to see him. And pay for a lawyer other than a public defender."

I took a deep breath. "How bad do you think things are for him?"

Waylon nodded curtly. "It's hard to say. He could get a fair plea deal, or he could end up in trial and end up with an unsympathetic jury. At this point, hiring him a criminal lawyer after his transfer is complete is the next step. He isn't a hardened criminal and I'm sure once he explains his reasoning, they'll understand."

Now more than ever I wished for a miracle, especially with a baby on the way. His baby. Our baby. It seemed so surreal. Then I thought. What if I went to Alaska? I had thought about writing him a letter, but telling him I was pregnant with his kid in a letter was too impersonal. That and I really wanted to see him. I really wanted to see him in the flesh, to see for myself that he was all right. More than anything, I wanted the truth.

"I want to go to Alaska to see him too," I said.

Waylon was taken aback. "What?"

"I want to see him." I repeated myself. "There is something I need to tell him, in person."

"What?"

I shook my head. "It's something I need to tell him. Something he deserves to know."

Waylon opened his mouth to object but surprisingly stopped himself. "Fine. Give me your number, and I'll call you with the details of when it'd be a good time to fly."

I nodded. "Thanks."

Waylon checked his watch. "I really have things to do, Danny. I'll keep in touch, but please stop showing up unannounced. It's attention I just don't need."

I nodded. "As long as you keep me updated, because I can be persistent and I'm sure Ian told you that too."

Waylon chuckled. "That he did."

Without another word I exited his shop, and ambled to my car. Next step was figuring out how I was going to afford a flight to Alaska, and for accommodations.

Then reality hit me like a ton of bricks. I was going to see Ian, also known as Brody for the first time since that morning. Would he want to see me? I never considered that until this moment.

16

Tomorrow, I board a plane to Juneau, Alaska. It has been fifty-eight days since I last saw Ian. I missed him so much, but I was so nervous to see him. During my ultrasound yesterday, I learned that I was officially eleven weeks and one day along. I sat in my car outside of the storage locker into which I had finished packing away most of my belongings. I had sold the last of my garments, even the medieval inspired one Ian had tried on. A lump took shape in my throat, threatening to swallow me whole. It seemed like everything was going according to plan, tied up with a neat little bow, but I was drowning.

A week ago, I got the phone call from Waylon. He was so matter of the fact. His voice rough and annoyed. He gave me a time to meet him at the airport. "Don't forget to book a ticket." I had fumbled, wondering if he was going to stand me up. I was so upset to find a one-way ticket to Alaska cost me nearly six hundred dollars I didn't have, but I reluctantly put it on my credit card anyway. I only had a couple thousand dollars after selling off some unneeded household things for when I landed in Alaska. But I needed to see Ian.

I drove home slower than usual. A few hours ago, I had handed over the keys to my tenants and dropped my car off with a friend to store for me. I wasn't ready to let my house go, but I couldn't afford to stay in it without any income. And I needed to see Ian. Every night since I found out I was pregnant, I imagined being in his arms again, drowning out all the lies and the pain he caused me. He wasn't a bad guy. Every decision I made since New Year's Eve had to have some purpose. I went against my instinct for most the year and now, in the brink of late fall, I was making the impulsive decision to leave my life behind.

I walked through the front door and gazed upon the blank canvas, which someone else would soon enjoy. Over the past week, I tediously examined dozens of applications. My Victorian house was my baby, and I didn't want any ol' person to live here. A year ago, the thought of renting the house would have seemed completely insane to me. The only thing going my way these days was that the rental market was solid. I snagged a young, professional couple in their late 20s. No kids. No pets. The rent would be enough to cover my mortgage, property tax, insurance, and almost the entirety of my car payment. I'd still have to come up with a couple hundred dollars a month for other living expenses, but I had a few months of car payments saved up until that became a problem.

I sat on the couch, which I was leaving for the tenants and stared at the four, blank walls. I had two large suitcases, my sewing machine, and a carry-on bag ready to go. I rocked back and forth, trying to keep myself calm. I had checked off every mental box multiple times, but I still felt like I was missing something.

I flipped through some of the last texts between Ian and I before his arrest.

I love you babe. Can't wait to see you tonight. That was the last night I saw him, the last night I knew him as Ian. When I arrived in the small town twenty miles from the airport, I was still struggling on how to approach him. Even after practicing saying "Brody" out loud several times, it still sounded so weird.

I look forward to it. That was the last text message I ever sent him. It was at break time, after a busy afternoon, and I was looking forward to hanging out with him. He mentioned earlier that day that his landlords were out of town. I hadn't slept the night at his place…until that night.

I liked to believe someone was looking over me that night. If the police stormed his house and found out he wasn't there, would they have eventually found him at my house? That would always be my fear, for any reason. But the possibility was so close.

I dialed his number, but it was disconnected. I didn't know what I was expecting. After his arrest, it only made sense all his assets in his dead best friend's name were seized. Literally everything he worked for was gone. I couldn't imagine how he was feeling, being behind bars, alone. Did he think I hated him?

The time ticked by slowly when a text from Kiera flashed onto my screen

What are you up to tonight? Are you out of your slump?

Texting between Kiera and I picked up again. We hadn't hung out since she and my mother ambushed me. Both of them didn't know about my sudden plan to up and leave for Alaska. Even I was still coming to terms with my impulsive decision.

I have a few things to do tonight. Maybe after.

I knew it was a lie. I wasn't going to see her before I left. She would know the instant she walked into my house that I was running away and she'd run to my mother. She hadn't been the supportive friend I thought she was and I couldn't risk letting her get in my way, even if I was going to miss her.

I hadn't even considered how I was going to break the news to my parents. Mom still wasn't talking to me. The few curt text messages she sent me were emotionless. How could she go from twenty questions to silence? I rubbed my slightly bloated stomach. Mom still didn't know about my pregnancy. My best friend didn't know and, most of all, the father didn't know. The unborn boy or girl connected Ian and I. I just wished things were under better circumstances.

Oh, come on. Let's go for coffee, go shopping, or something. You still can't be mad at me for being concerned. Besides you had long enough to mourn him...

She couldn't even use his name. Ironically, neither could I. I still had a good few hours before I handed over the keys, and what good was I staying put feeling sorry for myself. Maybe Kiera would be more forgiving.

Fine! How about coffee, as I really do have things to do!

As soon as it sent, I was regretting my decision.

Fine, café by your house in ten.

I sighed.

I shouldn't have agreed. "*Fine*" was code for annoyed. If I backed out now, she'd show up here and blow my cover. The consequences would be tragic.

I got into my car and drove to the parking lot of the café. I hadn't been here since his arrest and this would probably be the last time for a while, depending on how Alaska treats me.

A few minutes later, Kiera's Mustang pulled up next to mine. Kiera got out sporting a pair of yoga pants and an oversized hoodie. At least she had no plans to drag me to a bar.

Kiera flung her hair over her shoulder as she approached my car. "Long time, no see." She planted her hands on her hips as I got out.

"Hey," I said.

"It's about time you got out of the house. What have you been doing lately? I haven't seen you around the gift shop."

"I got a full-time gig, so taking some time off." It was the first thing to pop in my head.

"Let's go in and you tell me about this *gig*." There was hint of sarcasm in her voice almost like she knew deep down that I had lost my job. But I wasn't going to admit it to her.

I ordered myself my usual and sat by the window, in full view of the parking lot in case this was a trap and my mother showed up.

Kiera sat crossed legged on the chair, the most awkward position possible. "So? What is this gig? And how come I didn't hear about it until now?"

I scrambled for an answer. "I didn't want to broadcast it because of all the drama going on lately." I gulped. "It's just a client with a huge order." I hurried to think of something to embellish this fake job. "It has inspired me to work toward my own line."

Kiera smiled. "See, there is the Danyelle I know."

I grinned, as I snuck a quick rub of my belly. It was almost instinct at this point. "Yeah, it's been rough."

Kiera rolled her eyes. "There are other men. In a year, he'll be Ian who?"

I bit my upper lip but somehow kept my composure. If only you knew Kiera. If only you knew. "I'm sure you're right." I said in a low voice.

Kiera took a sip of her hot chocolate she had ordered. "Now, don't get all glum on me. I think what you need to celebrate this next step is to get laid. This weekend, we are going on a road trip."

"A road trip?" It was more of a statement then a question. If only she knew I was soon going to be on a plane going across the country. "This weekend is not a good time. But when I get more time, and my life more or less figured out." That last statement wasn't a total fabrication. I needed to figure out what my next plan was once I got to Alaska.

Kiera frowned. "Whatever you want, Mrs. Future Fashion Designer."

My phone vibrated. I glanced down at it. *Don't forget to be at the airport by 5am.*

Waylon.

"Who is that?" she asked.

"It's a client. I'm sorry, I need to go, Kiera." I didn't need to go right that moment but I wanted too. I was so close to just bursting at the seams. After how Kiera had been treating me, I still wanted to tell her everything. But I couldn't trust her, so I needed to leave.

"Fine!" Keira called after me. "I'll text you later, after you are done with this client."

Out in my car, I sat quietly as Kiera drove away. Relief washed over me. I didn't know when a friendship felt like so much work. We used to be so close. We used to be like sisters and I could count on her for anything. Was it worth keeping contact with her? Was it fair to ghost her like ghosting a fling?

It wasn't just my friendship I was leaving behind, I was leaving behind everything: my family, my house, and the city I grew up. In a few hours I was going to be homeless and that was a scary thought.

I felt my eyes water, as I sank into the seat. Change was never easy for me. If there was one thing Ian had taught me, it was to let go of the outcome. I needed to stop second guessing myself. I made this decision and I would own it.

Tomorrow I would be entering Ian's world. I would soon get a feel of where he grew up. I didn't know what to expect, but I was both excited and nervous to see him. How was he doing? Would he be excited to me? Waylon said he talked to him all ready, but wouldn't expand on what he said.

I took a deep breath as I pulled away. I hoped after this there was no more secrets. I hoped he'd be honest with me, let me in. Because I wanted to give him another chance, give us a chance and to give this baby a chance to have two loving parents. I just hoped he took the news well.

I arrived back at home, around five. I loaded up my suitcases inside my backseat and just sat in the driveway. Each time I went in and out, the harder it was to let go. Soon at 5:30, a blue truck pulled up. My new tenants.

They exited the truck, and we exchanged a few words, and I handed them the keys. The paperwork and deposit were exchanged days ago. It was final.

Now I was heading to my hotel by the airport to drop my luggage off, and to drop my car off in storage.

Tomorrow was a new day.

Tomorrow I would be that much closer to Ian.

17

Waylon and I landed at Juneau International Airport late afternoon. I knew he was going to make sure I got here safely, but had no idea he was going to fly with me.

Waylon only had a backpack on him, and was nice enough to help me with my luggage. "Do you have any accommodations?" he asked me. On the flight we didn't say much. He just told me he had made arrangements for me to see Ian, who was lodged in the next town's jail. The chief of the small little town where Ian was held was an old friend of Waylon's, and he arranged a little private meeting in close contact.

"I have a room near the jailhouse, I'm going to check out. Fully furnished."

Waylon nodded. "I'm going to be in town for few days if you need anything. Then I have to get back."

I nodded as he helped me cart my things across the airport and to the doors.

Outside the airport doors, was all white. I gulped. There was at least a foot of snow. The automatic doors opened, and a freezing breeze rushed in along with an older man who was bundled up in a hat, large parka, and snow pants.

Waylon pulled a toque and mitts out of his jacket pocket. "I see you didn't come prepared for an Alaska winter."

"I have a jacket with a hood..." I trailed off as I sighed to myself. Waylon was right. No, I didn't come prepared. I didn't even check the weather forecast for Alaska. I knew it was colder, but this was another thing all together.

Waylon rolled his eyes at me. "Once the rental company drops off my rental car, I'll take you to the store so you can get some proper winter gear. Ian wouldn't be pleased if he knew I didn't help you out."

"Are you going to continue to call him Ian now that the truth came out and all that?"

Waylon rubbed his hand through his long hair. "That is a good question, Dany. I've known Ian for a long time, so it'll take getting used to calling him Brody again. When I spoke to him on the phone, he said he was coming around to accepting it himself. It's change."

I glanced away. Change was an understatement. My whole life in the matter of a couple months. It was January, I was pregnant, jobless in the middle of a state, across the country in the brink of winter. I don't think I grasped just how much my world was going to change.

My phone vibrated and I jumped. I checked my phone, and it was a text from the lady I was supposed to go see. My heart stammered. What was I thinking even consider moving in with a stranger? I shook my head to keep my mind on my purpose. The rent would be four hundred a month. I think I could swing that. There were a few job openings around the place, too. I just wouldn't tell them I'm pregnant, and hoped they would be okay with it.

I stared at the time. "What time am I seeing Ian?"

"Six pm. So just over an hour."

"Okay, good. I have a place to look at in twenty-five minutes here."

Waylon nodded. "Just shoot me the address. As I said, Danyelle, I'll help you out while I'm here."

Five minutes later, the rental car showed up. Waylon prepaid the bill and insurance before loading all my stuff into the back seat.

I gave Waylon the address.

"That's walking distance from the jail. We should be able to stop there, and if it doesn't take long, stop to get you some better winter gears in time to reach the jailhouse."

Waylon pulled away from the airport parking lot, driving thirty on the slick roads. From the passenger seat, I stared out the window as he entered the freeway. Every direction was a sheet of ice, white, angelic almost. It was different from the city, the sunshine, and business.

I turned to look at Waylon. "Do you think Ian will want to see me?"

Waylon furrowed his brow. "He misses you. He asked me if you were mad at him."

"And what did you say?"

"Before I knew you wanted to see him. I told him you were in shock and dealing with it. I couldn't tell him how badly you reacted when you came to my shop."

"How do things look for him, legally?" I pressed further. I had looked up the criminal law in Alaska and it was a lot more lax than my state.

Waylon shrugged while fixating on the road. "His lawyer is trying to work him out a plea bargain. He has no criminal record, and has family here so hoping that will help."

"Family?"

Waylon hands gripped the steering wheel.

"It's fine..." I urged.

"It's complicated, and not my place to tell you. He had a terrible upbringing. I think it is something he needs to tell you when he is ready. I think he hasn't fully processed it himself."

I already knew all this. I knew he had a tough childhood, why else would he take his dead best friend's identity and move across the country to start a new life? I wanted to ask Waylon how he pulled it off, but I stopped myself.

A few minutes later, we pulled up to a small house. It was a midcentury house in much need of a makeover, but I didn't have much choice. I hugged myself as I got out of the car, my purse on my arm, and walked up the steps. I was five minutes early and I hoped the owner didn't mind.

I knocked on the door, and an elder lady answered it.

"Danyelle?" she asked.

"Yes." I nodded sheepishly.

She let me inside and showed me around. She stopped at a bedroom at the end of the small hallway. She opened it up. It was about half the size of my master bedroom. It had a twin-size bed, a dresser, and a desk. That could work for my sewing machine.

The lady mumbled off a few more things.

I nodded.

"So where are you from?" the lady asked me.

I explained how I just got out of a long term relationship, and decided to start fresh. I said I could pay two months' rent and a deposit, but I needed something right away.

She nodded. "You seem like such a nice young gal. I'm not sure why you chose these parts, especially coming from the other side of the country."

I nodded. She seemed sweet, and I just hoped she said yes and rented to me.

As we walked back to the front door. "Let me take a few hours to decide and I'll let you know after supper."

I smiled. "Thanks, I hope to hear from you."

I brisk walked back to the car, shivering. I was frozen.

"Damn it's cold," I muttered when I closed the door.

Waylon laughed and I shot him an *I'm not impressed* look back.

"How did it go?" he asked.

"She'll let me know in a few hours. She seems nice, and besides, it's only temporary."

"Well, we should get going. It's almost time for you to see Ian. That did take longer than expected."

He drove the two and half blocks to the jail house.

My heart sped up as he pulled up to the front doors.

"Just ask for Tony. He's expecting you. I'll be back in an hour to pick you up."

"Thanks," I said as I got out. "Do you mind if I leave my stuff with you?"

Waylon nodded as I got out.

I took a deep breath as I entered the doors.

I walked up to the desk. A man in a police uniform behind a computer barely made eye contact with me. "Can I help you?" He stared straight as his computer.

"Can I speak to Tony?" I asked nicely.

My legs felt wobbly as if I could crash to the floor. Never mind throwing up. So far, I had been able to hide my pregnancy from Waylon. But I couldn't hide it from Ian.

"So, you must be here to see Crane?"

It took me a moment for the last name to register but I manage a nod.

He laughed a little. "I'll let the sheriff know you are here."

The sheriff, a man in his late forties, with a full head of long black hair and full beard lead me down the hallway to a room. It was similar to the room; the police had interviewed me shortly after Ian's arrest.

"He'll be in here shortly," he said in a low gruff voice.

"Thanks," I said, before he left the room, the steel door closing behind him.

I took a seat on the uncomfortable plastic chair across from a metal table. An empty chair lay on the other side. Waylon had said he knew the sheriff and special arrangements had been made just for me. Normally, he had told me before we boarded the plane was that if it was anyone else, I'd be stuck in a room, with a sheet of plexiglass separating us, with only a phone to communicate.

My stomach churned, as I waited. The room was dark
and dungy. A single light bulb hung from the ceiling, and
bars hung over the window leading outside. A cold shiver
shot up my back as I shifted in the chair. I unfastened the top
button of my shirt, and rebuttoned it. My heart raced as time
seemed to slow right down. Why was I so nervous to see Ian?
How would he be? How would I be? There were so many
thoughts racing through my mind. Maybe I wasn't ready for
this. I felt the litter flutters in my stomach. It was a reminder
of why I was here. That and I still loved the man dearly.

Soon the door open, and I jumped out of my seat. There
he was.

Ian's eyes shifted to his feet, his hands handcuffed to his
front. I gasped a little too loud for comfort. He gazed
upwards, mouth upturned. He had a strange sadness in his
eyes. We stared at one another, without saying a word. My
upper lip trembled as I let out a weak hello and a little wave.

The guard uncuffed Ian, and lead him to the seat. "Shout
if you need anything," he said.

"Thanks," Ian mumbled to the guard.

I glanced at Ian, dressed in orange, sporting a full beard
and unkempt hair. "How are you?" I finally forced myself to
say. It was a stupid question, I realized, but someone needed
to break the awkward silence.

"Been better." That was his simple response. His voice
wasn't angry, but he didn't sound particularly excited to see
me. Maybe because I sounded so depressed.

"I missed you," I said with earnest. I hoped to loosen the
mood a little, hopefully get a little smile. "It's good to see
you." I added quickly.

Ian's left hand reached over and caressed mine briefly.
"It's good to see you too." He pulled away and his gaze
casted downward. "I-I never thought I'd see you again."

My heart split in two. "I'm here now," I said. "I won't lie,
though. It has been hard."

Ian shifted in his chair and played with his collar. "I'm sorry." He took a deep breath. "Why are you here after everything I did to you? You came all the way to this cold, shitty place?" He stopped to catch his breath, answering his own question, with another one. "For me?"

So many emotions ran through me. Ian was the picture of a broken man. It was so hard to see. I felt guilty for ever being angry with him, but a part of me still was.

"What should I call you?" I instantly changed the subject, but scared to even ask.

Ian shrugged. "Brody is my real name. There is no more pretending."

"How do you feel about it?"

Ian laughed, but it was mixed with melancholy. "What choice do I have? Real question is, how do *you* feel about it?"

"Confused..." I trailed off. "But it doesn't change how I feel about you. I love you. I care about you. And I'm not going anywhere."

Ian's eyes watered. "I love you, too."

We stood at almost the same time. I reached over and hugged him, tears running down my cheeks.

"There is something I need to tell you." I finally blurted out. I needed to tell him the truth, before I changed my mind. I was like a yo-yo. When would it stop?

Ian naturally parted from me and turned and sat back down. "Okay…what is it?"

My forehead dotted with perspiration. This shouldn't be this hard. All I need to say is three little words: *I am pregnant.* So why couldn't I?

"What's wrong?" Ian asked reaching over the table.

He was behind bars, concerned about me, and I couldn't just tell him. Practice what I preached which was honesty.

"Dany?"

I flinched and forced eye contact. "I'm pregnant."

Ian's eyes widened as he covered his mouth with his palm.

"I know it's not ideal," I tried to reason with him. I could throw up. The timing couldn't have been any fucking shittier, if I had tried.

He pressed a fist to his mouth, and let a deep labor breath.

Then there was a pause. "Please say something."

"How far along?" he mustered. He grimaced, and bit his upper lip.

"Eleven weeks," I replied.

He covered his hands with his face and mumbled something I couldn't quite make out.

"It'll be all right." I said out loud, in attempt to convince him but in reality it was probably to convince myself.

Ian laughed. "Yeah, how do you figure, Hun? You live across the country, and I am in jail."

I shook my head. "Not exactly…"

Ian burrowed his brow. "What do you mean?"
I sat there in utter silence. Anything I said would make him feel badly, but I couldn't lie to him. I couldn't pretend I had a job to go back to, a supportive family to take care of me, or even a house to live in. But maybe he'd realize how much I loved him. Maybe he'd finally open up and be honest with me. I could have kept him out of the loop, let him sit in here all alone thinking I didn't care. The decision on what to say next weighed on me like a ton of bricks.

"I kinda came here with long term in mind."

"You need to go back. You have family and support you just don't have here," Ian explained. "I am in no position to be there for you."

" Then tell me, why did I pack up everything? Fly here to be with you?"

Ian flew his hands up. " Why would you do that?"?"

"I'm not trying to make you feel bad. And I know you will feel bad. But I don't want to lie to you." The words spilled out. "I lost my job, my mother disowned me, and I found out I was pregnant all within a week of one another.

So, I made the decision to downsize, rent out my house, and hop on a plane. And here I am!" I wouldn't tell him I likely wouldn't have hopped on a plane if it wasn't for the pregnancy, nor did I ever want him to know I had almost ended it.

"Why?" he muttered. "I mean I'm glad you are here, but why? This is the last place you want to be. This place is cursed." He shook furiously. "You don't want to be here. You don't want to raise a baby here. Please hop back on a plane, go home, make up with your family and forget about me."

"No!"

Ian opened his mouth to object, but I put a finger to my lips signaling him to stop. He wasn't going to do this. It took me so much to make this decision I wouldn't let him try to waver my feelings.

"I said no. I'm not forgetting about you. I'm not giving up on you and there is no discussing it." I trembled. This was my decision and Ian wasn't going to change it.

Ian nodded his head. "I love you…not that I deserve it."

"I love you, too." I paused and took a deep breath. "But there is something I need from you."

"What? Name it."

"The truth." I sighed. "No more lies. No more secrets. Can you do that for me?"

Ian bit his lip, and shame crossed his face.

"No more lies."

He shifted in his seat. "Not in here. When I get out, I promise."

I found my face warm, as he was avoiding me yet again. "Ian?"

"I can't. Not in here. Please!"

Just as I went to object, the door opened.

"Times up," the guard announced gruffly as he approached Ian and told him to stand.

He cuffed Ian.

"I'll hold you to that, Brody."

Ian's face grimaced as he offered a weak goodbye.

"I'll see you soon, my love," I called as he was hauled out of the room.

I sat there for a moment reflecting on what just happened. Before I hand time to ponder everything, my phone vibrated. It was a text from Mom,

Where the hell are you? What the hell is going on? Answer me.

I didn't reply, and instead slid the phone back in my pocket. I still hadn't figured out what I was going to tell her yet. I had bigger fish to fry, such as finding me some stable income in this new town and maybe see a doctor.

I just prayed it all worked out. The door opened and I followed the sheriff to the front of the police station. Outside I saw a woman with long curly hair waving her arms in the air, while talking to Waylon. She stopped, looked at me with a look of familiarity, back at Waylon before she turned and walked away.

18

Thankfully, the little old lady messaged me back a few hours later and offered me the room. It was a check mark off the list of things I needed to accomplish before Waylon went back home. Now I needed a job, before I started showing. I had a few flowy, bold printed garments that covered that area without screaming I was hiding something, but that wouldn't last forever. I lay on the bed, which was too firm, and not comfortable like my mattress at home. I missed home, and my throat tightened just thinking about it, but I knew I made this decision and needed to own it.

My mind went back to last night. Who was the woman who talked to Waylon as I left the station? She had stared right at me, and something about her stood out. Almost like I knew her from somewhere and vaguely recognized her somehow. I wanted to ask Waylon who she was, but I didn't. At the time it didn't seem like my business, but the way she looked at me and walked away, it almost seemed like she was expecting me. Did Waylon say something to her about me? Did she know Ian? Why else would she be there talking to Waylon, act so shifty, then simply walk away?

I crawled out of bed and paced the small room. I felt so out of place, so worn out. It was eating me up inside. I just wanted to see Ian. I didn't realize that my visits were going to be scant. Waylon also didn't warn me that once he left, I might have to settle for no physical contact. I prayed that Ian got a favorable plea deal, hopefully before the baby came.

My phone vibrated. It was the fiftieth text from my mother today, mixed in with some frantic texts from Kiera. I hadn't gotten around to replying to any of them. I had all the time in the world, but what would I tell them? That I got up and fled across the country without telling anyone? They wouldn't understand. My good girl image was already tarnished.

Kiera had just sent me a long text: *Where the hell are you, girl? Everyone is worried about you. Some strange person is parked at your house. They said they lived there now. If you needed a roommate, why didn't you tell me? I would have helped you out, bestie. I thought you were over Ian. But turns out, you're foolishly pushing everyone away. Seriously? He is not worth it. I regret ever helping hook you two up. Now that nightmare is over, so come home from your vacation, and we'll find you a hottie to fuck. Okay byyye.*

I laughed at how stupid she sounded and how wrong she was. She didn't even know I was pregnant and had dropped everything and moved across the country. She had no freaking clue. She didn't know that every day I considered her less of a friend. The most devastating thing was that she used to be my best friend. She used to be the person I confided in. I tried to reconnect our friendship, but her true colors had been revealed.

I wanted so badly to text her that I already found my hottie. Ian was attractive, even if he was rough around the edges. But most of all, he was the father of my baby. He almost checked off every box I ever wanted in a man. He was hardworking, handsome, funny . . .

I can't do this anymore. I replied to her. Should I text more? I really just wanted her to go away. Our friendship was over, but I was too cowardly to just end it. I was playing games and I hated it.

Then let's go on vacation girrrrrl...

I sighed and rolled my eyes. I so badly wanted to blurt out where I was and what I was planning, but I couldn't.

I need some space from everyone. I don't need new hotties or vacations. I just need some time to figure out what I want in life.

I could picture one big eye roll followed by a sarcastic remark. Lately everything was one big joke with her. It was nauseating.

Whatever!!!!!!!!!

I couldn't take much more of this. I unpacked my laptop. Thank God for Wi-Fi being included in my rent. I needed to find a job. Waylon had said he'd seen a sign for a part-time cashier. I could do that, as long as I made enough to cover my rent and food. Here's hoping my renter doesn't destroy my house or skip out on rent. That'd be just my luck.

I had a resume that I'd made back home. Maybe I could get away with just changing the address. I would have to come up with an explanation of why I moved across the country. I had considered all the cons of moving here, no car and lack of high-paying employment among them. There wasn't even a museum or fabric store in sight.

I opened a document in a word processor and changed my address to this one. I stared at the screen like this was some kind of alternate reality. I wanted so much to go home, to my house, and sleep in my own bed. But I couldn't. I couldn't let Ian down.

I applied to a few of the job openings this little, isolated town had to offer. I just hope that "curse" Ian spoke of didn't haunt me. I needed a job.

I lounged back in bed once I was finished job searching. I checked my messages. One was from Mom from a few hours ago.

Now I know why you are avoiding your family. That was her response. Maybe Kiera messaged her or told her how I went on a little vacation. Mom was pissed, and I had no choice but to let it pass. Right now it was a blessing in disguise.

I'll talk to you soon.

I texted her partly to appease her and partly to keep them off my back. Eventually, maybe closer to my due date, I'd tell Mom the truth. But I also considered how that may be a problem. Mom would have questions. I needed to come up with a better cover.

There was a knock on the door. "Danyelle?" My new roommate called from the door.

I sighed silently and opened the door.

The elderly lady stood with a plate of cookies. "Here, my dear." She had a grin from cheek to cheek. I hadn't eaten today, so it was welcoming. "A little something for a new tenant."

I took it from her bony hands. "Thanks." I smiled.

The lady beamed. "I'll leave it for you. But do feel free to come out and make yourself at home. It's no life being cooped up all day."

I nodded and responded with a weak thanks. She was wise but didn't know me very well. The gesture was nice. Eventually I'd need to get out of this room and interact, go for a walk or something.

Just then, my phone vibrated.

I know you have been lying to all of us. You didn't tell us you lost your job and couldn't pay your bills. So you got a roommate. I'm ashamed of you. I didn't raise you this way.

I sighed. So Kiera did go to my mother. Only Mom wouldn't believe my wanting to be the next big fashion designer story. That and whatever embellishments Kiera added to the story.

I wanted so badly to text Kiera and tell her to fuck off, but I stopped myself. Why did I always stop myself? She had been treating me like shit, but I couldn't call her out on it. I wasn't one for conflict, and I wasn't going to be that kind of person.

I rubbed my stomach. The tie that brought Ian and me back together.

Have you talked to Ian today? I texted Waylon. I knew he was planning on seeing him soon, but if he wasn't, I wanted to. I missed Ian so much.

Yeah. He's going to call you collect here soon.

My heart got all giddy just thinking about it. I had to remember he was the reason why I was here.

Okay.

Then my thoughts returned to the woman outside the station. I wanted to ask Ian about it, see if he had any ideas about who she was.

My mind kept wandering. I wanted to know so badly what Ian was hiding. I'd tried so hard to call him Brody but couldn't do it. What if I say his name wrong and get those death stares? The last thing I wanted was to make life more difficult for him.

The phone rang. *Unknown number.* I was hoping it was Ian and not Mom or Kiera trying to get a hold of me.

I brought the phone to my ear. "Hello," I whispered.

"Do you want to accept a call from Brody Crane at County Correctional facility?"

I answered and entered my credit card number.

"Hello, Love."

It was him.

"How are you?" I asked. After how awkward our visit was, I wanted to be careful, but I couldn't help but add, "I'm glad you called."

"Waylon just left." There was a pause. "I'm sorry. I told him about the pregnancy. I hope you aren't mad."

This time I was silent. I guess I wasn't ready to tell him, but I shouldn't be surprised. Ian confided in Waylon about everything.

"What did he say?"

I could hear Ian's breathing in the background. "Congratulations. Not much else. But I know him well enough to get that he wasn't too thrilled."

I nodded even though Ian couldn't understand. "It isn't the best of circumstances. But how are you feeling about it?" Ian hadn't said much since our visit was cut short.

"I don't know, Dany. Honestly, I feel like a failure." There was a strong dismay in his voice. "I don't know what is happening with my case, never mind how am I going to support a baby . . ."

"I understand," I said with much sadness.

"I'm sorry," Ian reiterated. "I'm sorry for lying to you. I'm sorry for agreeing to be with you at all. I dragged you into this mess and I wish I could go back."

"There is no going back." I took a deep breath. "I guess the question is, do you want to be with me?" The regret hit as soon as I asked it. But I didn't know how Ian felt; he never openly said he was excited to get out to be with me.

"Of course I do."

"Then I'll wait. I applied to a few jobs today. I'll figure out a way."

Ian breathed heavily into the receiver. "I wish I could hold you right now."

A few tears formed in the corners of my eyes. "Me too, Ian."

I wanted more than anything to jump through the phone and hold him in my arms.

"Dany?"

"What?"

"You need to start calling me Brody," he replied in a low voice. "That is my legal name."

"Okay," I replied tautly.

Two minutes left. A robotic voice responded in the receiver.

"We don't have much time left," Ian said.

I hated having to spring it on him over the phone, but I wanted to get it off my chest.

"When I left the jailhouse, I saw Waylon talking to a woman. She looked at me, and she looked familiar. Do you know who she could be?"

"Did she have curly hair, dark brown eyes, and a glare that could make your heart jump a beat?" Ian asked.

"Yeah."

"That's my mother. Violet Crane." Ian sounded so sure. "But don't expect much."

I wanted to say something, but the robot spoke again, stating that we only had thirty seconds left.

"I love you," I said. "I'll talk to you soon."

"Love you too, Dany. I'll call you tomorrow."

Before I could muster a response, the phone call ended. I lay back on the bed.

His mother?

He said her name was Violet Crane. I didn't expect him to tell me anything, but not only did he tell me exactly who she was, but he was so curt about it. He said not to expect anything, but he knew me well enough to know that I would search her. Unless he wanted me to search so he didn't have to talk about her.

I retrieved my laptop and entered Ian's mother's name and the state of Alaska into the search engine. The first heading said: *Juneau Resident Violet Crane Sentenced in Robbery.* It was dated three years ago.

I clicked on the link and a mugshot of the same woman I'd seen appeared. She had straight, long black hair, and those same intense, dark eyes. The type of woman I wouldn't want to run into after dark. I saw the resemblance between her and Ian. I glanced away a moment. If only I had done more of a search on this when Ian told me about his friend going over the edge, I could have put two and two together sooner.

I looked back.

Violet Crane, 46, pleaded guilty to one count of robbery in the second degree as part of a plea deal and was sentenced to two years in prison.

Damn, I thought. I backspaced and did some more scrolling. I clicked on a few more headings.

Violet Crane, 44, was arrested and held on a $500.00 bond for shoplifting.

So she has a thing for stealing.

Violet Crane, 43, was arrested for solicitation and was released.

I deleted my search bar and type up public arrest records for Alaska. She'd had a few charges in just the last few years, so I wondered how many there were against her in total. Based on her age, she would have been born in 1970.

It didn't take me long to find her name. I searched through her arrest records, going back to 1991, which would have made Ian only three.

I counted seven theft charges, a drug charge, a few prostitution charges, and an assault charge. Most of them resulted in probation.

So she was a career criminal. Her most serious charge was the robbery. Even after Ian went *missing,* she spent more time committing crimes than being there, looking for her son.

While she was out doing stupid things, who was looking after Ian? She didn't sound like a very responsible mother, but that still wasn't a reason for him to leave his family behind. I knew he felt guilty over his friend's accidental death.

I closed out of my browser and sat back. Ian was right; I shouldn't have expected much. I wasn't super surprised, because anyone who doesn't actively look for their son, even if they were presumed dead, was someone who wasn't warm and concerned.

As much as Mom wasn't pleased with me, I know she'd be all over the news looking for me. She wouldn't give up. Just thinking about my mom left a sour taste in my mouth. I also felt guilty lying to her. Until this whole thing with Ian came out, she was supportive.

What did Ian have?

I squeezed my eyes shut, clenching and unclenching my fists. I felt like throwing up. The world around me was spinning. The reality of this shitstorm came full force. I had left my whole life and support system to come to Alaska, and Ian . . . I mean Brody Crane . . . came from nothing. He had nobody except Waylon.

I couldn't study Ian's face when he told me his mother's name after I told him Waylon and his mother were talking. Were they friends? Or maybe Waylon was just defending Ian?

I shook my head, reprimanding myself. Brody. His name was Brody. He had to learn to live by his birth name, and I needed to learn it, too. My baby was going to be a Crane.

I bit my upper lip. I still had time left, but I hadn't thought much about preparing, beyond saving money. There was insurance I still needed to get, a name for the baby, clothes, and a bigger place.

Then I pictured my baby, visiting his or her father in prison.

And I sobbed.

19

Three weeks in this god-forsaken state, and every day felt more awful than the last. I found a job in a little coffee shop, a ten-minute walk from my place, and I started last week. Every morning I dragged myself through a foot or more of snow and back again. I spent most of my time alone, in bed surfing the internet, or visiting Ian, who in my head would always be Ian, but to the outside world, he was Brody Crane.

I sat at the desk, staring at my sewing machine. I had sewn nothing in weeks. After paying for a phone bill and insurance, I had very little left for anything else. With a baby coming in twenty-five, I wasn't sure how I could afford that.

My tenant made a money transfer today, and by tonight the mortgage company would take that too. I kept wondering if my house was in one piece. I fell in love with that place when I moved in. I tried not to think about it, but I was homesick. I missed my car, my house, sewing, and even my family.

The highlight of my day was the once a week visit I had with Ian and the daily phone call, which didn't always come.

Even Mom hadn't texted me in almost a week. My excuses and reasons why I wasn't around much weighed down. My tenant luckily, had reported no harassment or problems. I don't know what I'd do if a pipe burst or something worse, except having to pay on credit to fix any problems.

A knock on the door brought me out of my floundering. "Yes?" I called.

"I was going to head to the supermarket. Would you like anything?" the owner called through the door.

"No, I'm good, thanks for asking," I shouted back. I realized I probably sounded rude, but I was too lazy to get up. I was too busy thinking and overthinking to make any additional effort.

I peered out the window as she waddled through the snow to her running car.

A thickness in my throat emerged, signaling the onset of a stream of tears. I stooped my shoulders, my hands limp. I had lost all my desire to do much. I pulled out my cell and logged onto social media. I scrolled through pictures of back home, the ocean, the nightlife, and all the cultural. I missed it all. I wanted so much just to fly home, but I couldn't. I had to be here for Ian. I set the phone beside me and hugged myself in a fetal position. I should be thinking about the bright side and thinking about this baby. He or she was a blessing, but it didn't feel like it. I kept replaying the clinic in my head *what-ifs* flew around in my head like a bird searching for its prey.

I closed my eyes, trying to fight these thoughts. I had to see the light at the end of the tunnel. I had to remember the positives. Alaska had some of the laxest laws in the country, and he didn't have a criminal record. Ian was a good guy, he was kind, affectionate, and we got along so well. Soon we would be together, and I couldn't wait. I smiled as I remembered all the good times we had. All the things that should have prevented us from being together didn't stop us. Was this a sign? Was this the last obstacle we'd have to face?

We are celebrating our one year anniversary. It wasn't the romantic setting I pictured...

My phone rang, and I opened my eyes. It was Ian. After I accepted his call and inserted my credit card, I quickly said, "Hey.".

"Hey, Babe," Ian said. His tone of voice was different this time. It wasn't exactly upbeat but wasn't dejected.

"What's up?"

"I was offered a plea deal," Ian said.

I sat up. "And?"

"My lawyer thinks I should take it, but I wanted your opinion."

I shook my head. I wasn't a lawyer, so why the hell would my opinion matter. "Why?"

"If I plead guilty to three felonies I get one hundred days in jail, subtracting time served on remand, one hundred hours of community service, and two years of probation. I could be out in two weeks. My lawyer doesn't think I'll get a better deal."

"Then take it," I said. "What's there to think about?" He had already spent so much time in jail, and what was a few more weeks. I just wanted this to be put behind him.

"One of the conditions of the probation is I can't leave the State of Alaska."

"Small price to pay for freedom," I blurted immediately.

As confident as I sounded, I was secretly dying on the inside. I didn't want to be here. I didn't want to spend two years in this cold, depressing place, but I didn't say anything. Ian, being locked up for years, was always a possibility. This way, he could be free, he could be here for the baby, and we could be together. Where he would go was still a question. Where would he find work?

"But what about you?" Ian said, his voice low.

"I'm not going anywhere," I said. "I just want you out, and we can figure it out."

I heard his deep, labored breath. "I am not sure what I'm going to do. No one is going to hire a felon who has identity theft on his record. I have no marketable skills."

I wanted to say, 'you are a plumber,' but bit my tongue. He was a plumber, under a different name. Under Brody Crane, there wasn't much. He had to start over with nothing. I'm sure Waylon would help him out as best as he could, but Ia – Brody, I reminded myself for the millionth time - was in a tough spot. But surely someone would have to give him a chance, or maybe he could open up his own business.

"Everything will work out," I said. I needed to keep his spirits up.

"I hope so." There he was, back to sounding dejected again. "I can't wait to see you. I'm going to take the deal, and in a few weeks, these four walls won't separate us, will they?"

"No, they won't,"

"How are you feeling?" Ian finally asked. "How about the baby?"

I was caught off guard. "What do you mean?"

"How is the baby? I hadn't asked much about the pregnancy, and I feel bad that I haven't been there for you."

I shrugged, even though he couldn't see it. "I felt bloated, hungry, and wanted to stay in bed all day. Baby has a heartbeat." It was the only positive highlight I had experienced this pregnancy. I heard the thump, thump, thump, and saw the little flickering of its heart.

"That's good," he said.

"You'll be out for the next ultrasound, where we find out it's a boy or a girl," I quickly added. Despite how shitty things have been, I was glad to finally be able to enjoy the next stages of this pregnancy, now that Ian would be able to experience them with me.

"That's exciting. At least there is that."

I smiled. "See, not everything is as sad as it needs to be."

"Very true."

I heard a beep on my phone. It wasn't the usual narrator telling us our phone call was ending. "There's someone on the other line."

"Answer it," Ian said. "I want to get a hold of my lawyer anyway about accepting this plea bargain."

"Okay, talk to you soon," I said sadly. "Love you."

The beeping kept annoying me.

"Talk to you soon, Love."

Then click.

I sighed as I switched to the other line without even checking the number.

"Hello!"

"Danyelle!" Mom shouted on the phone.

"Hey, Mom." I sat up. "It's nice to hear from you. How are you?" Her tone caught me off guard.

"Where are you?"

"I'm in the library, downtown." I quickly replied. "Why what's up?"

There was a loud sigh, and some background noise, but I knew she was seething. "Stop lying. Where are you?"

"I am —"

"I'm at Juneau Airport. Now tell me where you are, so help me, Danny, don't make me find out on my own!"

My eyes widened as my face turned hot. *No! No! No! She can't know.* I rocked back and forth while loosely holding the phone.

"Where are you?" Mom repeated.

"I needed to get away," I said. I was hoping she'd turn around and hop back on that plane and go home.

"You ran right for him? After everything, he did to you? Now I'm here to take you home, don't argue with me."

I opened my mouth to speak, but she interrupted me, just like she always did.

"You are coming home. Now tell me where you are; otherwise, I'll make things very hard for Ian…or Brody or whomever the hell he is."

I panicked, rose, and paced. "I'll be home in a few weeks," I lied. I tried to save face. She couldn't know where I lived. How did she even know where I was?

"Last chance, Danny."

"Fine…" I said. I shot off the address. "Just don't make a scene. I don't want to upset the owner."

"What about your house…?" Mom trailed off. "Never mind, I don't want to know right now. Now you better be there when I get there." Then she hung up on me.

Are you kidding me? I hugged myself and paced. She was a good hour, at least from here. I just hoped she didn't come to the door. How would I explain to Luna about my mother? What was I going to say to my mother in general?

I looked down at my bloated stomach. I had a small frame, so it wouldn't be much longer until I couldn't hide the pregnancy.

I rubbed my palms together, and then through my hair. I needed to get myself together. I changed into a long sleeve shirt and jeans. I had to appear as if I wasn't hanging on by a thread, even though I was dangling off the edge.

I exited the bedroom and down the narrow hallway to the living room. I tended to come out here when the house was empty. I helped myself to some milk and a few pieces of fruit. I didn't buy a lot of groceries as I was saving for my baby.

I was a penny pincher, but I was desperate, and every single penny I spent needed to be toward a need. My wants and my luxuries, were nonexistent.

I plopped down on the sofa in the living room and picked up a newspaper. I scanned the front page, with an apple in hand. A winter festival this weekend. That could get me out of this house if I somehow don't get forced back home. I swallowed hard. There was an assault and a DUI last night in this town. There wasn't much else — at least no mention of Brody or his legal issues.

I sat the paperback where I found it as I finished my apple. How was she going to react to my pregnancy news? Was she going to freak? My mind spun as time sped on by at a million miles an hour.

Forty-nine minutes later, a red car, I'm assuming a rental car, appeared in front of my new house. Mom soon after exited the vehicle, underdressed in just a sweater and jeans. Dots of sweat formed on my forehead as I headed for the door to meet her.

I didn't want to be around when the landlady returned home. I didn't want my cover story to be blown and to find myself being kicked out. I grabbed my coat, slipped on my boots, and headed outside.

Mom stood several feet from the front door. She said nothing, her face rosy red. I couldn't really tell if it was from her anger or from the cold or both.

"Hi, Mom…" I mumbled with a lot less poise than I could muster. I've never felt so low in my almost twenty-seven years on this Earth.

She stood akimbo a few feet away. "Do you know how furious I am, Danyelle Rose?"

I nodded. What else could I say? Anyone within view could likely feel the tension in the air and be able to cut through it with a knife.

Mom rubbed the back of her neck. "I had to come across the country to come find you because you couldn't stop lying…" She studied my face as if she expected some kind of response, but frowned when I remained quiet. "I thought you just needed some time to get over that, that thing, but then you started with the lying! I went to your work looking for you, and they said they had let you go. So what were you doing all this time? Sitting at home pining over the man who brought shame to our family?" Her jaw clenched as she paced in a manic state. "Where did your morals go? What the hell is wrong with you?"

I bit my upper lip, forcing myself to remain silent. This was the start of a familiar conversation or more like a lecture Mom had with my sister years ago.

"Yet, you stand there shamefully and can't even look me in the eye and defend your choices." She paused to take a deep breath. "It's because you let your family down. You embarrassed your father and me; you even brought that fraud into our home. We welcomed him! We trusted your judgment because you were always that smart girl. You had all the potential in the world. Smart. You were never in trouble and made good decisions."

Mom's face contorted as she opened her mouth but stopped as tears ran down her face. "You aren't even my daughter. My daughter wouldn't do this. She wouldn't date someone who didn't have a license; she wouldn't introduce someone dishonest to her family, and surely wouldn't drop her life and run across the country for fraud. She just wouldn't do that. So please enlighten me, Danyelle. Why are you? Why did you run across the country for a man who lied about who he was? Who came from such an unsavory background? This man made you abandoned your job, your home, and made you a dishonest person. So why? Please make me understand where the hell my daughter went."

"I didn't abandon my house." That was my simple response. Out of everything I could say, I could think that was the thing I spilled out. "My bills are covered."

It took every ounce of my being to keep a confident front when on the inside, I was dying. I made this decision. It may or may not have been the right choice to get up and run after my boyfriend. But I made it. I made the decision to lie to my parents, and I made the decision to be by Ian's side.

"Who cares about your stupid house? Stop avoiding the question."

I gritted my teeth. "Listen. I didn't abandon everything. I just didn't tell you where I was going. That is why you are upset."

"Excuse me?"

"I'm freezing." I shut her down. "I'm not talking about this in the snow. So let 's go somewhere else and finish this conversation?"

"The smartest thing you had said since I got here," Mom said, as she headed toward her car. I made sure the door was locked before I reluctantly followed her. I wanted to go back inside, crawl up in a little ball, and for Mom to go back home.

I got into the car; my nerves shot up as I was giving her some power when she was so angry. She drove slowly down the road. "And of all the places you run off too, it had to be snow and ice. Unbelievable."

My posture was stiff. "It isn't ideal, but it is what it is," I replied.

"Is he threatening you?" Mom asked as she pulled into a parking lot. Her face softened a bit. "If you are scared, then we can work through this." Mom rubbed her hands on her face and let out a deep breath. "After reading about how the real Ian Fogg went over the cliff, what a tragedy that was, I didn't put two and two together that maybe he was involved. That explains everything."

"He wasn't involved..." I said the tension in my jaw throbbed. "He's not threatening me, and I'm not scared for my life. I came here on my own free will." I glanced downward and then back at my mom's horrified face. "I lost my job..." Then I froze at the part of the story I didn't want to disclose. "Then, I made the decision to come to Alaska. There were some things I needed to figure out."

"What happened after you lost your job? What could possibly possess you to run for him?"

"I missed him..." I said. "I needed answers from him that I could only get by coming here. I just needed to get away. I made sure every 't' was crossed, and 'i' was dotted before I hopped on a plane. "I found a place, found a job, and am just waiting it out until the right time."

"And you couldn't write him a letter? Or call him on the phone? Oh, that's right because nothing about him is honest. I'll hire a private investigator if you want the truth. But my god, pack your shit and let's go home."

I placed one hand on the inside door, ready to run.

"What are you hiding?" she said. "If you don't give me one good reason why you are here, I will make it my mission to make sure Ian or Brody or whomever the hell he is, life is a living hell. I'll protect you when you don't even protect yourself."

"So you are going to alienate everyone in your life because you don't agree with them? You're going to threaten people because you aren't getting your own way. Do you ever wonder why no one ever goes to you for advice, Mom?" I shouted out. "They avoid you because you are overbearing."

Every one of my siblings tiptoed around Mom and did everything she wanted, in order not to risk her wrath. I put up this front, pretended to be someone I wasn't to please her, and she couldn't handle it when I did the opposite of her expectations.

Mom's mouth was agape. "If that is how you feel..."

"It isn't just me, Mom. I'm not asking you to like my choices, but you can't do this. You can't just hop on a plane, follow me and tell me what to do. I'm not a child anymore."

Mom shook her head, biting her upper lip. "You'll understand one day when you have a child of your own."

That lit a fire under my ass. "That is exactly why I'm here..." I blurted out. "I'm here because I'm pregnant."

Mom got out of the car. For the first time since I could remember, she was at a loss for words.

This could get interesting.

20

Mom dropped me off last night after I dropped the bombshell without saying a word. She texted me saying that she needed to comprehend this new development. My baby to her was like some kind of unwelcomed milestone on a large project. I knew she was furious, and I could imagine her sitting in a hotel room pacing, her face beat red as she schemed what she thought I'd need to do. I dodged a bullet for now, but Mom would rear her head again; today, most likely. She wouldn't let this go easily.

I sat at the kitchen table eating a bowl of cereal. Luna sat in her big recliner, snoring with the newspaper sitting on her lap and the television on a Sunday morning talk show. My gaze fixated toward the window and a new layer of falling snow. The visibility of the scant houses was almost nonexistent. I was glad I didn't need to go out there unless of course Mom decided to 'stop' by. She was stubborn and angry so if she wanted to barge in here to 'finish' our discussion she would. I hell bent intended to tell her next time she came to go home.

I took another mouthful and scrolled through social media, not that I expected to see much. It was really a slap in the face that I was in the middle of extreme cold when I could be sun gazing on the beach. As soon as Ian, I mean Brody's, probation was finished, we were going back. It didn't need to be that city but we would go back to where it was warm. I couldn't wait.

A text came across my phone, stumbling me out of my thoughts. It was from Waylon.

I'm in town and we need to talk as soon as possible.

I sighed. First Mom shows up unexpected and now Waylon. I just hope he didn't bring bad news, especially so close to his release.

Okay!

I kept my text simple. He had been so tight lipped about everything and what the hell his connection with Ian really was. I decided long ago not to give him anything without receiving something in return. Beside it seemed like he expected things from me and would never return the favor. Ian, for whatever reason, didn't want to tell me what the hell happened all those years ago.

I'll pick you up in five. So be ready.

Geeze. Didn't leave me much time to prepare, did he now? I was dressed in pajama pants and a tank top, which did accentuate my bump. Waylon already knew I was pregnant so no point hiding it.

I quickly washed my bowl, put it in the drying rack, and grabbed my jacket from the closet. Luna had gone above and beyond making me feel at home. I waited by the door, glancing out the window, shuffling from foot to foot, waiting. With a minute to spare, he showed up.

I ambled outside, quietly closing the door behind me. He was in yet another rental vehicle. The cool wind hit me like a ton of bricks. I still wasn't prepared for this weather and it showed. I got in the passenger side, slamming the door a little too hard for comfort.

"What's up?" I asked.

"Do you know who Sharla Fitzgerald is?" he asked.

I took a deep breath and sighed. How did Waylon know my mother? *Mom, what the hell did you do? What kind of drama are you cooking up now?* "What did she do?" I asked Waylon, afraid of what I'd hear.

"She has been requesting to see Ian. Do you know who she is? Ian is freaked out, but won't tell me who she is."

I bit my upper lip. "She is my mother." I wanted to curl up in a little ball and die. Why did she have to be here? Why does she want to see Ian? He had a reason to be scared. My mom was relentless. "It's all right as long as he keeps denying her visits." I didn't know what else to say because I wasn't sure yet how I was going to convince her to leave.

"Well, Violet... I mean Ian's mother... saw her and I had to explain to her I had no idea who she is. Then after she briefly saw Ian, you got brought up."

"Did she see Ian before or after I saw him for the first time?" I remembered back to her, staring at me as I walked out of the jailhouse three weeks earlier.

"Before, why do you ask?"

"Because I caught her staring at me, after the two of you were having quite a cozy conversation." I found myself wanting to roll my eyes. I don't know what he expected from me. "Honestly, I want to know how you really know Ian," I blurted.

"It's complicated."

I clenched my jaw. "You seemed to know Violet very well. Did she know Ian was missing all this time? Or what is it that you aren't telling me?"

Waylon shifted in his seat. "Why don't you ask her yourself?" Waylon glanced out. "She has requested to see you."

A cold chill shot up my back. But what could she possibly want from me? Then there was the risk of Mom stopping by my place. There was too many variables and risk that I wanted to say no.

"I could tell her no, but that woman is a talker."

I raised an eyebrow. "A talker?"

Waylon lower his gaze. "I'll admit I've known Violet for over thirty years. Her relationship with Ian is complicated. That is why I can't tell you anymore. So what do you want me to tell Violet?"

"Sure whatever." I sighed. "I'll meet her."

I was curious. If I said no, I'd likely think about the what ifs and want to know who Ian's mother was. Ian had dinner with my parents, so how bad could it be for me to meet his mother?

"I'll text her right now."

I shifted in my seat. Maybe I could have waited until Ian told me the truth. But there was no going back. Besides, I had some questions of my own. The question was, would I have the confidence to ask them? The biggest one at the moment was *what the hell were you doing when your son went missing*? She spent time committing crimes rather than searching for him, hanging missing person posters, or doing news interviews. I know if I had a son, I'd always be there for him. I'd protect them like a mother should.

And how the hell did Waylon fit in all this. Ian and him had this unusual bond, and it was enough that I assumed Waylon followed Ian or Ian followed Waylon across the country. But why?

"Okay it's all settled," Waylon said as he pulled away from the curb. I almost realized we actually didn't leave the house yet.

I brushed some uncombed hair out of my face. Would it have hurt to at least brush my hair? I wondered what my future, possible mother in law would think of me. I pushed that thought to the back of my mind. *Don't expect much!* Those were Ian's words. Those were words he used to explain his own mother. I wondered what kind of relationship they had or would have now that he was back home.

"Don't over think it," Waylon said as we pulled up into the parking lot of a local café. Thankfully it wasn't where I worked. I didn't need that aggravation.

Waylon got out of the car, and I followed suit. I fidgeted on the spot. He looked around, when he stared right at a rusted car pulled into the parking lot. It stopped and out stepped out the woman I saw the first day.

She was medium height. Her curly hair was pulled back into a ponytail that cascaded down her back. Her face was pale, freckled, concealed with a shade of lip stick. As she moved closer her deep, dark brown eyes which resembled Ian's in shape, approached.

"So this is Danyelle," Violet said, looking me up and down like a fresh piece of meat. "Seems like a nice looking girl, I'll give Brody that much."

"Violet?" I said.

"Yup." She held out her hand, which I reluctantly shook. "I'm sure Brody had some choice words to say about me." Her response was cold. She didn't seem particularly upset about it, it was so matter-of-fact.

"He didn't say much at all, honestly." I would leave out the *don't expect much* part of our brief conversation about her.

Violet nodded. "So, Waylon, why don't we go in?"

I stood there awkwardly. It was almost like I wasn't even there. She talked to me but then talked about me as if I wasn't even there. Mom would be interrogating at this point of the meeting.

I followed them into the café.

"Order me a coffee," Violet told Waylon, who didn't scuff at the blunt response as he went and got one. No one asked me if I wanted anything. So I reluctantly sat across from where Violet sat.

"So?" Violet said with a twisted smile. "You and my son...?"

I looked at her with a blank stare.

She laughed. "So you're the serious type, hey. It's okay to loosen up."

"Um, I don't follow?" It was true I was serious, but I didn't understand what she was saying, never mind finding humor in it.

"You are just not what I was expecting, that's all. It's really nothing," Violet said as Waylon returned to the table.

"What were you expecting?" I asked.

"Someone less serious. Don't take it as a complaint."

I prodded at the sleeves of my jacket. "I guess."

Violet turned her focus to Waylon and whispered a few words to him. Waylon looked at his phone and back at me. "I have a call to take. I'll leave you two." He got up and headed for the exit.

Great, he was leaving me here with her.

"So what did Brody really say about me?"

I looked at up at her. My leg trembled.

"Now, don't lie now, dear. I just deserve to know what he had to say."

"He-he said not to expect much from you."

Violet took a sip from her hot beverage and rolled her eyes. "Of course he did."

I straightened. "Why is your relationship with Brody strained?"

Violet flinched, maybe from not expecting the question, or because she wasn't used to people questioning her.

"A breakdown of communication. I never was able to bond with him the way I should've, I guess. But he didn't make it easy either."

I opened my mouth in awe. Was she blaming this on Ian?

"Don't act so surprised, sweetheart. I'm sure Brody wasn't the most open and outgoing guy you ever met. He did lie to you about who he was. The truth was he was always like that. He kept things in. I tried to visit him, but after ten minutes he told me to leave. I have to respect that."

I almost rolled my eyes back at her. My mom wouldn't respect that. If she wanted to see me, which was evident since she got on a plane and followed me here, she would get her own way. "No, he isn't much of one to open up, right."

Violet swung her arms in the air. "See, I think you know enough about him to know why our relationship isn't that good."

I could picture why. She gave a I *don't give a fuck* vibe. Her son was missing for ten years, and she made a half-ass attempt to see him. How did Ian feel? Rejected. He likely just wanted his mother to put more of a fight up to see him.

"Do you even want to really reconnect with him?" I realized now it was a rude question, but that was her son.

Violet glared at me. "Look, honey. You can't make people want to be in your life. I'd love to have a relationship with him but I'm not going to beg him. All I got out of him during our ten minutes, if it was even that long visit, was that he didn't need me, he was fine, and that he didn't know why I suddenly cared now."

I felt bile raise in my throat. I thought my mom being overbearing was bad, but this was sad. Violet didn't sound the least bit upset about her son accusing her of not caring. Did she not care at all why he ran away, or why he didn't want to see her? What kind of childhood did he have?

"Does Brody have any brothers or sisters?" I asked. Maybe she could fill me in on some family history.

"Yeah, he has younger two brothers. One is in jail, one moved somewhere in Texas. I know you're going to ask so going to just tell you… I don't know exactly who his father is."

Damn, I thought. Two of her sons were in jail, and two of them ran away. I guess she wasn't mother of the year.

"Danyelle!"

I jumped to find my mom standing there by the table. I felt myself shrink to a few inches.

"Hey, mom," I said in as cheerful voice at possible.

Violet turned and looked at my mom. "Hello, so you are Danyelle's mother. I'm Violet. I take it you met my son, Brody."

Mom's face frowned.

"So I get where Danyelle gets her seriousness from."

Mom faked a smile. "Yes I met *your son*... What an actor he is."

Violet shrugged her shoulders. "I guess he needed to be to hide who he really was."

Mom plopped down next to me. "So Violet, assuming that is your real name..."

"Do you need to see some ID?" Violet responded calmly.

Mom body tightened. She normally held her composure really well, but I don't know if she'd be able to right now.

Heck, I wasn't sure if I was going to stick around for this showdown. I trembled, silently beside Mom.

"Did you know what your...your offspring did to my family?"

Violet glared at my mother. "The same thing he did to his own. What is your point?"

Mom bounced her right leg. "I should expect he'd be raised by someone like you. To lie, to pray on women with class."

Violet rolled her eyes. "You are acting like he killed somebody. Look, I thought he died. I had no idea he ran away to another state. What would you like me to say?"

"Nothing..." Mom bit her upper lip. "But it does say a lot about you."

Violet finished her drink, and tossed the empty cup on the table next to her. Mom's eyes followed it with astonishment. "I don't know what is stuck up your butt, but I'm not responsible for whatever choice he made. He deceived us all. He made the decision and now he has to live with the consequences. Just like his friend Ian did when he stole my son's car and drove over the cliff in it."

"What kind of mother would you need to be for your son run away without telling anyone?"

Violet reached in her pocket, and took out some lipstick and a mirror. "Isn't that what Danyelle did?" She didn't even look at me, and I said nothing. "I've sat here for ten minutes with you, it's obvious you don't like my son, and I can almost guarantee you wouldn't have been okay with your daughter travelling across the country to see her delinquent boyfriend."

"At least she isn't changing her identity," Mom spat back.

Violet stood up to leave. "Does it really matter?" She straightened her back. "You can't control your kids. Just like Brody chose to run away, your daughter - whether you like it or not - ran away, too. We may have come from two different walks of life, but we are the same. We have kids who, for whatever reason, felt the need to run." She started to walk away. "It was nice to meet you, Dany, and congrats on the pregnancy."

She walked away. I sat there frozen, shocked. I didn't tell her about the pregnancy, and she didn't once mention it the entire time I was sitting here. She was as nonchalant about it as she was about everything else. She wasn't the least bit fazed about anything my mom said.

I stared at my Mom, who was noticeably pissed. "So when did you tell *her* about your pregnancy?"

"I didn't?" I said, still staring at the door, which was long vacated. "That was the first and only time she even mentioned it." I wondered if Ian had told her. Then I sighed. I never got to ask her about Waylon and what his connection to Ian was. Why Mom? Why did you have to show up here?

"Pack your bags. We are going home right now," Mom announced suddenly. "There is no way I'm going to let that woman around my grandchild."

I shook my head. "No!"

Mom went to grab my arm, but I pulled away and headed for the door. I wasn't a child. Violet was right about one thing: you can't control your kids. Mom couldn't control me, and she was right that I ran away.

"Stop right now, Dany, this instance."

"Or what?" I said on the sidewalk outside the café. "I'm not leaving. That is the end of it."

Mom opened her mouth and took a deep breath. "I spoke at length with your father last night. We both are in agreement you aren't equipped to raise this child here. You have a father who is in jail, and from the looks of it, a grandmother who doesn't give a shit."

"I'm not leaving," I repeated myself.

"I'm not asking you to leave, Danyelle. Your father is on his way here right now, and together we are taking you home. You may not like it, you may not agree with it, but it is happening."

I turned and walked away.

"Don't walk away when I'm talking to you! This is precisely why you are coming home, and why we will fight for custody of our grandchild until you grow the hell up."

I turned around, hands on my hips and glared at her. "I *am* walking away. I won't be boarding a plane with you, and you won't get custody of my baby." I accentuated each word with force. "I'm sorry you are upset with my decision. I'm sorry you are finding it hard to accept my decision. But until you do, we will no longer have any contact. That includes coming to my place of residence or my place of work. Also no texting, phone calls or I'll file a harassment complaint."

Mom face turned a deep red. "I guess you leave me with no choice…"

"And if you do anything to hurt Ian or make it so he doesn't get his release, I'll make sure you never see me or the baby ever again. Now leave me alone before I call the police."

Without another word, I walked back into the parking lot where I saw Waylon sitting in his car, staring right at me. It felt so good to stand up for myself. I hated it had to come down to threats, but she was disrespecting me. She was trying to control me, and I wouldn't have it.

I got in the car and slammed the door. "You can drive now!" I told Waylon.

"Violet told me about your mother."

"She won't be a problem," I replied. "It's just sad I never got to ask Violet about your connection to Ian."

Waylon didn't respond as he took me back to my place. I was about to get out of the car, annoyed at the resistance, but stopped. "I don't get why it needs to be this big secret. You care more about Ian then his own damn mother does."

"I was there the night the real Ian drove over the edge."

"Wait, you were there when his friend drove over the edge?" I interrupted.

Waylon choked on his words. "I watched as my only son plummeted into the ravine. At first, I thought it was Brody, but when I found out it wasn't, and found out about his plans to escape Alaska, I helped Brody out."

"How?" I asked.

"Before they discovered Brody was missing, we flew to Fairbanks. We hid out there for a few weeks. Brody had taken all Ian's ID with him. His birth certificate and his social security number. Ian never had a driver's license. After they pronounced who you now known as Brody was deceased, 'Ian' told me he intended to leave Alaska and leave his old life behind. I didn't know he used the birth certificate to apply for a driver's license." Waylon paused. "I would have convinced him not too if I had known what his true plans were. I thought he wanted to just get away for a few months, then go back home and tell everyone he was actually alive."

I sat in silence as I took it all in. "So you ran away with him."

Waylon shook his head. "More like I lead him there. I booked a flight for myself two months before he came. I established somewhere for him to live. I used all my savings to open up shop then had him come over. I treated him like a son, I guess, in a way to help fill the gaping hole for the son I lost."

Waylon stared downward, a tear ran down his face.

"I'm sorry to hear about your son."

"Thanks," Waylon said and smiled. "I should get going."

I wanted to ask him more, but stopped and got out. "Thanks."

He waved as he drove off. It all made sense. All of it. He felt guilty that he couldn't save his son, so he took Ian under his wing. But the big question floating around in my head was, why did Ian run? Why change your entire identity?

 I guess the rest of my answers would have to wait until after a nap, something to eat, and for Ian's release.

21

Today was Ian's release.

All last night I couldn't sleep. Life had finally settled down after Mom went back home. She didn't even say goodbye, which for the both of us was probably best. I only found out because my former best friend texted me.

You're throwing away your family for that convict. Why didn't you just come home with your mother and grow the hell up?

Thankfully, I had grown a backbone with my mother, so I easily replied. *And I'm ending a friendship over it, too.*

My father and I had a quick phone call when my mom wasn't around, but all he said was, "I love you and wish you'd reconsider." He even didn't respect me enough to stand up for my mother. I doubt now if he was even on his way to Alaska. I told him I'd visit. But if he wasn't willing to stick up for me, he and Mom were a packaged deal.

I spent the last hour staring in the bathroom mirror, deciding which way to style my hair. Ian, who I was still trying to come to terms with as Brody, wouldn't mind, but I did. I braided my hair. It had grown a couple of inches, and it was long enough that it cascaded.

I bounced from foot to foot, as my emotions were all over the place. Soon Ian and I would be reunited. I was still sad we would not be living together, not yet at least, but I knew our time would come, and hopefully soon.

"Waylon rented me a room for a few months for me until I get on my feet." That was what Ian told me a few days ago over the phone.

It wasn't ideal, but I didn't have enough money yet to move out of Luna's house. So we'd have to make do with spending time with each other in other ways. I could hardly believe in an hour he'd be released. We'd be reunited, without the constraints of that place.

I put the brush down. My hair had a part slightly off to the right and I concluded that was good enough. He really wouldn't care, and our relationship wasn't perfect, so why should I try to be?

My jeans were getting tight, so I was stuck in sweats and tank tops that were skin-tight, or an oversized sweater. I still had a few of Ian's he had left before his arrest.

I paced back and forth. What would be the first thing I'd do? Hug him? Stand there like an idiot waiting for him to make the first move?

As I headed down the hallway, Luna came the opposite way.

"You look like you're in a good mood." Her eyes twinkled as a broad smile appeared.

"I'm pretty decent," I said with a smile. "You as well."

"Well, happiness is contagious." She winked, then smiled.

I didn't say anything as my face grew hot. She exited into her bedroom, closing the door. I ambled toward the door.

I grabbed my jacket and boots and walked outside. Today's forecast said it would be 'warm' by Alaskan standards, but still too damn cold for me.

I dragged through the snow, another four inches had dumped last night, and it would only get worse in the next few days. I keep telling myself that Alaska would get a summer, eventually. I would get some sunshine finally.

When the sidewalk ended, I walked on the street as cars pushed their way passed, probably driving at only 10 miles an hour or so.

I stopped just short of the station. All the tension left my body. My heart raced, and my body warmed. I was so excited to see him.

Ian walked toward the door, wearing a sweater and holding a garbage bag. He smiled from cheek to cheek, and his eyes widened in wonder. I set his bag down beside him as I ran and we embraced. He was free.

I pulled away finally, staring him deeply in the eyes, touching his chest, as happy tears filled my eyes.

"I'm so glad you're out," I said before I leaned in and kissed him.

"Me too," Ian said as we embraced again. Warmth infused my body. A tingling surge started in my chest and spread outward, my stomach fluttering and heart racing. I was so glad to see him; so glad to leave where we left off.

Ian reached into his jean pocket and pulled out a piece of paper and a key.

"What's that?" I asked.

"This is the address to the room Waylon rented for me."

"Where is it at?"

He listed off the address.

I grinned. "That isn't far from my place," I said. "Just up the block."

"Perfect," Ian said. "It will only be temporary until I can find employment. Waylon seems optimistic I'll find something.

Apparently some people in this cursed town feel sorry for me. Let's hope that means someone will give me a chance."

"Well, let's hurry and check out this room, Hun, because you aren't dressed for the weather."

Ian shrugged. "It's not bad."

I stared at him like he had grown an extra head "It's freezing out here!"

"Welcome to Alaska…"

He said nothing else before he began to walk away from the station. He speed walked a bit, gently pulling me along. I was slow, cold, and always tired it seemed. He glided me along without so much as looking at signs. I shouldn't be surprised since he spent two-thirds of his life here, and here he was.

"Here it is," he said. We stopped at a two-story, mid-century bungalow. I followed him sheepishly to the door. He knocked.

"Brody," a man said when he answered the door.

"Yes," Brody said.

It felt so weird hearing that name. I tried to so hard to get used to it but he'd always be Ian to me.

"It's the last room on the left. There is a mini-fridge for your use," the man said.

I followed Ian passed the man into the house. It smelled like faint cigarette smoke mixed with a floral air freshener smell. The house was cramped, outdated, and looked like it was right out of the sixties.

I followed Ian to the bedroom. It was small. On the floor were a thin mattress and a dresser with a mini-fridge on top.

Ian didn't say anything as he put his bag on the floor.

"It is only temporary," I said.

I didn't need Ian to say anything because I assumed he was thinking what I was thinking.

He sat down on the floor, and pulled me into his lap, wrapping his arms around me. "Anything's better than jail," he whispered. His heartbeat fast, and his breathing heaved. "I just never thought I'd ever end back here again."

I nodded. "I know."

Ian shifted his position. "Waylon told me you met my mother."

I glanced downward because I hadn't told him. "Yeah. He also told me about Ian and how they are – were - related."

He took a deep breath. "Waylon dealt with a lot of guilt. We were drinking, all three of us. Waylon wasn't a good father to Ian. He bought him booze, drugs, whatever it was, you name it." Ian twisted his upper lip. "I didn't know he took my car. I was too drunk to stop my best friend from going over that ravine. I replay the day back in my head repeatedly. I didn't know until a week later that Waylon saw it happen. He saw the car over the cliff."

I stroked his hand. He flinched. "It's not your fault."

He didn't speak.

"It isn't your fault. It was an accident and I can't imagine how you must feel. I can't imagine how Waylon must feel."

Ian released me, and I sat down off his lap. He stood and paced. "It was the camel that broke the back. It was the thing that put me over the edge. I had nothing left here. I had a mother who didn't give a shit about me. I had a brother who pushed an elderly lady down a flight of stairs."

I jumped. "What?"

Ian sat in front of me. "My younger brother was sixteen when he pushed our neighbour down a flight of stairs. He was high on meth. He ran away and was arrested the next day. Our mom didn't even show up to his arraignment."

"What happened after that?"

"She died three days later in hospital, he plead guilty to manslaughter and was sentenced to thirty years."

"I'm sorry," I muttered, reaching out to stroke his hand. He tensed but didn't pull away. "You don't need to tell me anymore."

"I promised I'd tell you the truth," Ian muttered. "I'm tired of living this lie. After spending four months in jail, and almost losing you and everything I am done running. I'm done pretending that life never happened."

His tone broke me. I can't imagine what the hell he had to endure to want to run away. Tears formed in my eyes. I felt so bad for him and everything he had been through.

"Three days after I was transported back here, my mom requested a visit. I thought maybe, just maybe, she'd be happy to see me. I shouldn't have gotten my hopes up. She showed up there, hungover. She didn't even hug me. She sat down and told me it was about time I dealt with the consequences." He choked on his words. "She didn't tell me she loved me, she didn't tell me she missed me. She just sat there. Cold. Calculated. She never changed. She didn't give a shit. So I told her to leave." Ian glanced downwards, his eyes jaded.

"I-I…" I fumbled to find the right words to say. But what could I say? I grew up with an overbearing mother, and he grew up with a mother that didn't give two shits. "So was she always like this?" I blurted.

Ian shrugged. "Yeah, pretty much. She often left my brothers and I with whatever random man she was dating at the time. We moved around all the time. I probably lived in half the towns in this cursed state. It wasn't until I was eleven when she finally settled somewhat. She hooked up with a man twenty years her senior." Ian gagged. "She was checked out."

"I understand now," I said.

"Understand what, Hun?"

"I remember back to when you met my parents. How you told me to embrace it."

He frowned. "I was wrong for saying anything. It wasn't my place."

"How so?"

"I assumed I knew better. I assumed I knew your parents subconsciously better than you did. It wasn't my place to tell you my opinion."

I took a deep labored breath. "It turns out I don't even know my parents." If there was anything I learned from Ian was to stand up for myself. I was too busy walking on tiptoes, trying so hard to please everyone, Mom in particular that I lost myself.

"Me neither," Ian admitted. "Me neither."

There was a silence in the room for a minute. "At least you have Waylon."

Ian's eyes widened. "Yeah..." He sounded sad, unsure.

Why I didn't know? He and Waylon were close for as long as I've known Ian. His mouth slacked, as his posture stiffened.

"What's wrong?"

"I hate her so much..." Ian mumbled.

"Ian, I mean, Brody, who are you talking about?"

"My mother..." His face turned a deep red. "When I was seventeen, I found her journal. I debated reading it, because I was afraid of what she may say. She was so cold, so detached on the inside, I suspected she had to have had an outlet somewhere."

"Meaning?"

"She wrote everything. She wrote how I was a cry baby. Or how she couldn't wait until I moved out. It was pages of pages of everything I wronged or refused to do..."

I sat there as I listened to Ian list off all the cruel things his mother did to him. She didn't give a shit on the outside, but it was clear she did. She cared. Just not in a good way. She didn't seem like she even wanted to be a mother. It broke me in half. I couldn't imagine being like that. Distant, cold, cruel and emotionless toward a child.

"I found out she had an affair with Waylon."

"Oh?" The word slipped out of my mouth. I knew they knew one another, but didn't know they had a relationship – if it could be called that.

"And she wrote that Waylon was my father."

I froze on the spot at the bombshell. "Your … father?"

"Only Waylon doesn't know that," Ian admitted. "Mom had lied so many times. She slept with so many men. What if she was wrong? I don't know if Waylon could take another hit like that. So I spent all these years keeping that knowledge inside me."

It was no wonder why he was so close to Waylon. Why he had no problem running to him when he needed help? It was because he was, or he strongly suspected that was his father. It was no wonder he was so closed off from everyone except him. Was I the exception? Did he let his guard down for me? My heart conflicted. If that were true then I was special, but what if that ultimately led to his arrest. What if he slipped up?

"I tried to run away from it all," Ian said. "I kept to myself, didn't let anyone close until I met you." Ian smiled slowly. "You taught me how to trust again. You taught me how to love again."

I embraced him. "I love you."

"I love you too." He nestled his head in my shoulder. "I thought I was doing the right thing by Ian, by running away. I wanted to leave my life behind. I thought if I took Ian's identity I could be the son Waylon lost. He could have his son back without the risk. I could have the father I never had. I could leave it all behind. So, I assumed 'Ian.' I fulfilled every dream he wanted. I went to school and became a plumber, I paid my taxes, and stayed out of trouble. I adopted a new me. Except it wasn't..."

"What do you mean?"

"I couldn't be who I was around you. It wasn't fair to you. I was a fake. I had to watch what I said. I had to keep everything inside when all I wanted was for you to know who I really was. Then I began to slip."

I nodded.

"You gave me another chance. Why?" Ian blurted. "Why did you follow me to Alaska?"

"Because I wanted to," I said. "Now that we have a baby on the way, it feels … right."

Ian pulled me close and kissed me.

"I promise not to let you down, again," Ian said as he kneeled in front of my stomach and caressed it. "And I promise you, I'll be the best father I can be. I won't ever let you down."

I "And I promise to love you," I said. I don't care about who you are, or what you did. I just want you to know, that I'm here for you. I love you."

Ian got back to his feet and gazed deeply into my eyes. I wrapped my arms around him and we stood in tranquility. I'd hold him to that promise, and despite the mystery surrounding him, I know he'd do the same for me